Impostors at
Blue Heron Lake

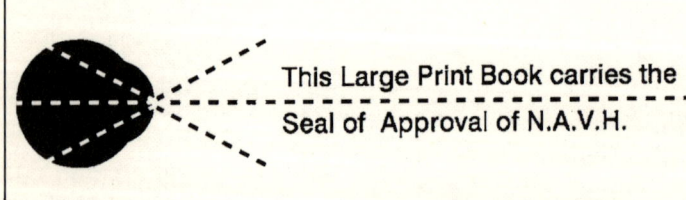

MAINELY MYSTERIES, BOOK 3

IMPOSTORS AT BLUE HERON LAKE

A ROMANCE MYSTERY

SUSAN PAGE DAVIS AND MEGAN ELAINE DAVIS

THORNDIKE PRESS
A part of Gale, Cengage Learning

Detroit • New York • San Francisco • New Haven, Conn • Waterville, Maine • London

HUDSON BRANCH

GALE
CENGAGE Learning

Copyright © 2009 by Susan Page Davis and Megan Elaine Davis.
Scripture taken from the Holy Bible, New International Version®, NIV®. Copyright © 1973, 1978, 1984 by International Bible Society. Used by permission of Zondervan. All rights reserved.
Thorndike Press, a part of Gale, Cengage Learning.

ALL RIGHTS RESERVED
This book is a work of fiction. Names, characters, places, and incidents are either products of the author's imagination or are used fictitiously. Any similarity to actual people, organizations, and/or events is purely coincidental.
Thorndike Press® Large Print Christian Mystery.
The text of this Large Print edition is unabridged.
Other aspects of the book may vary from the original edition.
Set in 16 pt. Plantin.

LIBRARY OF CONGRESS CATALOGING-IN-PUBLICATION DATA

Davis, Susan Page.
  Impostors at Blue Heron Lake : a romance mystery / by Susan Page Davis, Megan Elaine Davis.
    p. cm. — (Mainely mysteries ; bk. 3) (Thorndike Press large print Christian mystery)
  ISBN-13: 978-1-4104-3305-3
  ISBN-10: 1-4104-3305-6
  1. Maine—Fiction. 2. Large type books. I. Davis, Megan Elaine. II. Title.
  PS3604.A976I47 2011
  813'.6—dc22   2010043110

Published in 2011 by arrangement with Barbour Publishing, Inc.

Printed in Mexico
1 2 3 4 5 6 7 15 14 13 12 11

DEDICATION

To my dear husband, Jim.
Thirty-three years and counting.
Thank you for everything. I love you.
                                  Susan

To Adrienne, one of the best friends
I have ever had.
You are honest, supportive, and great:
my DLF with a very big heart.
Always remember "mine inheritance"!
And I will always remember
the cashew bars.
                                  Megan

1

"Wow." Emily Gray climbed out of her car and took in the Edwardian cottage standing on the edge of the woods. She'd seen Stella Lessard's home from the road many times over the years, but she'd never been this close.

Dried pods clung to last year's withered climber bean vines wrapped around the spindles of the railing on the sagging porch, and a few stray daffodils poked their sunny heads around the edges of the front steps. The paint on the front of the house was peeling a little, but Emily still thought the place was beautiful.

Stella had lived in Baxter for many years and was now in her sixties. She was a member of the Baxter Historical Society and the Friends of the Library, but that was about all Emily knew about her.

Her future mother-in-law had tipped Emily off about the cottage's claim to fame.

Nate's mother, Connie Phillips, had told her that about 125 years ago, Maine writer and nature enthusiast Sarah Orne Jewett and her friend Annie Fields had spent a few days at the cottage while returning from a trip to Quebec. En route to Sarah's home in South Berwick, they ran into a terrible snowstorm and took shelter at the little house on the shore of Blue Heron Lake.

After Emily heard the story, she asked Stella for an interview. Mrs. Lessard had owned the house for about thirty years and, according to Connie, was herself a Sarah Orne Jewett buff. Emily worked for the small local newspaper, and she thought the story would make a great photo feature for the *Baxter Journal.*

At first Stella was reluctant to grant an interview, but when Emily promised not to print anything she didn't approve of, the older woman agreed.

Emily took a deep breath. *I shouldn't be nervous. She's probably a very nice lady.* After grabbing her notebook and camera bag from the car, she walked to the house and knocked firmly on the door. She waited, listening for any movement inside.

Maybe she forgot about the interview. Emily looked around. Stella's ten-year-old

Toyota sat in the yard, but everything was still.

She moved to one of the windows on the porch and peered inside. The curtains were not fully drawn, and she could see into the living room. There was a green leather armchair to one side of the window, and was that a piano? Shadows filled the dim room.

After a while Emily knocked again. Still no answer. Was Stella hard of hearing? Normally, Emily wouldn't enter someone's house without permission, but because she knew Stella expected her, she tried the doorknob. The door was unlocked, so she opened it carefully and stuck her head inside.

"Hello!" she called. "Stella, it's me, Emily Gray! Are you home?"

She waited, but no reply greeted her. Even in the small town of Baxter, surely nowadays no one would leave home without locking up. Maybe Stella was asleep.

Experience had taught Emily that sometimes checking up on people to make sure they were okay was more important than social rules. *It's my responsibility. She doesn't have any family.*

Emily stepped into the front hall. The smell of hot tomatoes and basil permeated the air, and a faint light glowed from the doorway in front of her. She thought she heard a rustle.

"Stella?" She made her way toward the next room. "It's Emily. I'm here to interview you for —" She stopped short as she stepped into the kitchen. Tomato sauce was sputtering over the edge of a large cast-iron pot on the stove. And in the middle of the floor lay Stella Lessard.

"Stella! Are you all right?" Emily stepped closer but could see already that the old woman's face was a stark white. Her chest didn't rise and fall. Emily knelt beside her and felt for a pulse. Pulling out her cell phone, she hit her fiancé's number on speed dial.

He answered after only one ring. "Hi, Em. What's up?"

Emily sat back on her heels. "I'm . . . I'm at Stella's house."

"Oh, yeah, you had that interview, right?"

"Nate, I think Stella's dead."

"What?" His tone changed immediately. "Are you okay?"

"Yes, but —" Emily heard a noise. She stiffened, listening. Something moved in the next room. "Nate, there's someone else in the house."

"Em, where are you?"

"In the kitchen," she whispered. She inched into the far corner of the room, behind the edge of the stove, where she would be out of sight from the doorway. "Stella's lying on the floor, and I heard something in the other room."

"Well, get out! Fast! I'm on my way over."

Another soft thud came from somewhere in the house. Emily didn't stop to strategize. She dashed into the entry, through the front door, and down the porch steps. As soon as she was in her car, she locked the doors. She raised her phone to her ear, panting. "Are you still there, Nate?"

"Yep. Are you all right?"

"Yes. I'm in my car now."

"Good. I'll stay on with you until I get there."

"I think she's dead, but I couldn't tell for sure," Emily said.

"Hang in there. I'm only a few minutes away, and I radioed for the ambulance. Was there any blood?"

"No, I didn't see any," Emily said. "I suppose she might have fallen or had a heart attack."

"You're sure there was someone in the house?"

"Yes, I'm positive. Unless she has a dog or a cat."

Just then she heard a bang, like the sound of a screen door slamming shut, and a second later a figure she thought she recognized dashed from behind the house into the woods.

"Nate, hang on!" She opened the car door and shoved her phone in her pocket. "Cedar!" She ran along the side of the house, after the retreating form. At the edge of the woods, he turned and looked back at her. Sure enough, it was Cedar Sproul, a reclusive man who cut firewood in the winter and sold it to Baxter residents.

Emily slowed to a brisk walk, hoping she wouldn't scare him away. "Cedar, wait. It's me, Emily Gray."

His eyes narrowed as he surveyed her. "You're that reporter girl."

"Yes. Did you know my parents when they owned the paper?"

He nodded. "That was in the olden days."

She couldn't help giving him a weak smile. "Why are you running away?"

He stood in silence, and Emily wondered if she'd been wise to approach him. But Cedar was harmless. Everyone in Baxter knew that.

"Did you see Stella in the house?" she asked.

After another moment, he nodded and

looked away. "I came over to do some work for her this afternoon. She told me she wanted the banking all cleared away from around the house and her flower gardens raked up."

Emily glanced toward the cottage. Straw had been banked around the edges of the foundation. In front, it had been removed where the early flowers bloomed, but the back and sides of the foundation still wore their winter coverings. "I came to talk to her about the house," she said. "I was going to write an article for the paper."

Cedar licked his lips. "Guess that was you that came in. I found her lying there, but . . . when I heard you, I was afraid. I didn't know who was coming."

My feelings exactly! She nodded. "It's okay, Cedar. I called Nate Holman. You know Nate, from the marina?"

"They say he sold it."

"That's right. He and his mother are selling the business to Jon and Allison Woods. Nate's a sheriff's deputy now. I telephoned him, and he's on his way out here."

"Okay." Cedar raised his arms a few inches and let them fall to his sides again. "You want I should wait?"

"Please do. Nate will want to know how things were when you . . . found her."

Cedar's gaze slid away from hers. "She ain't breathing."

"Yes . . . I know." She pulled her phone from her pocket. "Nate? You still there?"

"Yes! Where were you?"

"I'm okay." She heard a motor approach and tires crunching on the gravel driveway. She turned to Cedar. "Come on. Nate's here." She took a few steps toward the front of the house then looked back to make sure he was following her. Into the phone she said, "Glad you're here. Cedar Sproul is with me. I'm hanging up."

Nate waved at her from inside the sheriff's department car as he pulled up in front of the house.

Nate inhaled deeply and sat for a moment to collect his thoughts before opening his car door. How many times had Emily scared him half to death, making him think she was in danger? Somehow, the woman he planned to marry attracted crime. This past year, it seemed she collected murders, almost the way some young women collected linens and teacups for their hope chests.

Thank You for keeping her safe, Lord. Emily and Cedar waited near Stella's front steps. Nate climbed out of the car and straightened his shoulders, keeping his eyes on Cedar as he walked toward them.

"What happened?" His gaze skimmed Emily. Her blue eyes were huge, but she seemed fine. "Who got here first?"

"I think Cedar did," Emily said. "Oh, and something's cooking on the stove. You may want to turn it off before it burns."

"All right. You two wait here. She's in the kitchen?"

They both nodded soberly. Nate pulled in a breath and went inside. He hated to enter the kitchen and disturb anything, but there was always a slight chance Stella was not beyond help. Besides, the heavy scent of spaghetti sauce held an acrid tinge that told him it was scorching.

Stella Lessard lay just as Emily had described, on the floor before the stove. She wore a bib apron over dark slacks and a yellow blouse. Her glasses were still perched on her nose, and her short salt-and-pepper hair framed her face. Her pale cheeks were spotless, except for a small orange smear he suspected was tomato sauce. A wooden spoon coated with the stuff lay on the floor between her and the stove.

Nate stepped cautiously over her legs, shut the burner off, and moved the kettle to one side. Then he turned and knelt beside the woman, checking for a pulse at her throat. He'd trained for this part of the job but had never yet responded to a report of an unattended death. He held his breath and concentrated, hoping, but felt no throbbing of her veins.

When he emerged from the house a few minutes later, Emily and Cedar stood right where he'd left them. He shuffled wearily down the steps. "I called the medical examiner."

Cedar raised his chin. "She *is* dead, then?"

"Yes, but we need a medical person to say so. They'll send a hearse out from the funeral home."

Emily reached for his hand. "I'm sorry, Nate. I wish we could have helped her."

"You did the right thing. And I'd say you were both too late to do anything."

Cedar sniffed. "I was just going to do the yard work that she wanted. Do you think I should take the straw away?"

Nate shook his head. "Leave everything just the way it is for now. We'll find out if Stella has any relatives."

"I don't think she's got no children, and her husband died a long time ago." Cedar's shoulders drooped. "She's been all alone for some time, yes, sir."

"We'll find out for sure." Nate took his

small notebook and pen from his pocket. "Was the front door unlocked when you arrived today, Cedar?"

The older man looked at him blankly. "Don't know. I went to the back. I knocked, and Stella didn't answer, so I looked in. Saw her there." He shook his head. "I didn't think she'd mind if I went in. But she wasn't breathin' none."

Nate wrote as he talked. "And then what?"

"Then I heard someone yell, 'Stella!' It jumped me, I'll tell you."

Nate saw Emily's lips twitch. "What did you do?"

Cedar looked down at the ground and kicked at a pebble. "I hid in the cellar way."

Emily's eyes flickered.

"Anything else you want to tell me, Em?" Nate asked.

Her golden hair caught the rays of sunlight filtering down through the trees. "The front door wasn't locked. I opened it and called to her, but she didn't answer. I smelled the food cooking and went on in to see if she was okay. That's about it."

"All right, I guess you two can leave if you want. Cedar, I may come around to see you and talk about this again."

"I'll be at my place. I ain't goin' nowhere."

Nate watched Cedar amble toward the

road and his small house that lay less than half a mile beyond Stella's, along the wooded lane. "Sounds like you and Cedar about scared the stuffin' out of each other."

"I thought I'd die when I heard that noise," Emily admitted. "I'm sure glad I had you on the phone. After what happened last year . . ."

"Right." Nate put his arm around her and walked her toward her car.

"At least Stella Lessard wasn't murdered."

"That we know of," Nate said quietly.

Emily stopped and stared up at him. "Oh, come on. No blood, no wound, no strangle marks. You don't think . . ."

"No, I don't, but we can't rule it out until the M.E. says it was natural causes. You know that."

She nodded, still frowning. "I don't think I'm ready to testify in another murder trial, thank you." She shuddered, and Nate squeezed her. Both had recently taken the stand in Superior Court as witnesses in the trial of Baxter resident Henry Derbin's killer.

"I don't expect that's a question here, but we'll know soon enough."

"I wonder who we can get information from to write the obituary."

Nate reached to open her car door.

"Maybe Felicia will have some ideas." The owner of the twice-weekly *Baxter Journal* knew everyone in town. Another thought occurred to Nate. "Oh, and ask my mom. She's known Stella since she came here, and Mom ran the post office all those years. She might know if there's any extended family."

"Good thinking. She'd know for sure if Stella ever got postcards from a cousin in Albuquerque or anything like that." Emily stood on tiptoe and lowered her eyelids.

Nate smiled as he bent to kiss her. Sweet Emily. His childhood sweetheart, soon to be his wife. "I love you," he whispered. "Don't let this bother you too much."

"Thanks." She hugged him one more time, got into her car, and drove away.

Nate turned back toward the little house. He used the time to examine the front porch, entry, and living room carefully. He saw nothing suspicious but discovered an old, free-standing safe hidden in a niche behind a bookcase. After another glance into the kitchen, he slipped up the stairs and made a quick search of the two bedrooms, bath, and large hall closet up there. Nothing out of the ordinary, but he realized how superficially he knew Stella. In the spare bedroom, he found an exercise treadmill and a quilting frame. The only photos on display in the other bedroom were one of Stella and Edgar Lessard's wedding and a framed snapshot of Edgar in fishing vest and hat. Nate looked at it and replaced it on the bedside stand. A leather shoulder purse rested on the bed. He opened it and found Stella's keys, which he took with him down the stairs.

His vigil was mercifully short. The Aswontee ambulance arrived first. Nate told the EMTs he had responded to an unattended death and that he expected the medical examiner soon. They entered the house with a portable heart monitor, made a quick assessment, and concluded there was nothing they could do for Stella. The medical examiner arrived just ahead of the hearse, and the EMTs left.

After his initial evaluation, Dr. Morse told him, "Most likely it was her heart. I'll file my report next week."

Nate saw him out and let the funeral director and his helper load the body.

His supervisor, Deputy Ward Delaney, drove in and stood with Nate as the hearse left. Together they went through the house. Since they were quite sure Stella had no relatives in Baxter, Ward made a list of items he felt the sheriff's office should hold for safekeeping, including Stella's purse, some bank statements and other records from her desk, her keys, and the contents of the safe.

"I didn't see a will." Ward handed Nate the clipboard with the list.

"If there is one, it's probably in that safe," Nate said. "But I didn't find a combination in her desk, either."

"Yeah. We may have to take the whole thing with us. Somebody stole a safe from the pharmacy in Aswontee last month. We can't leave it in the house not knowing what's inside."

"Too tempting, once word gets out that she's dead and the house is empty," Nate agreed.

Ward grimaced. "I hope you're feeling chipper — that thing's going to be heavy. I'll back my truck up to the door."

"I could get a dolly from the marina."

Ward bent and tried to lift the edge of the safe, testing its weight. He grunted and stood up again. "Good idea. And ask Jonathan if he can come help us."

An hour later, Ward drove off with the safe, leaving Nate to lock up the house. He threw the bolt on the back door from the inside. Going through to the porch, he locked the front door and pocketed Stella's key ring. As he walked toward his patrol car, Nate looked around the yard once more.

There was no wind, but at the edge of the woods, among the young green birch and maple leaves, he saw a flicker of movement. Nate shivered and focused in on a shadowy form just inside the tree line. The figure melted back into the trees.

Cedar. What was he doing here again?

Nate got into the squad car and headed for town.

2

Pastor Jared Phillips, or "Dad Phillips," as Nate now thought of him, set the water pitcher down on the table. "Why don't you kids sit down," he said to Nate and Emily. "We're nearly ready."

"It sure smells good," Nate said, trying to sound cheerful. He felt bad for Emily after her scare that morning, and his mother had seemed a little shaken by the news as well.

"It's your grandmother's recipe," said Connie, as she placed the platter of corned beef, potatoes, carrots, and cabbage on the table. "The best New England boiled dinner you'll ever eat."

They sat down and the pastor offered a word of prayer.

When he opened his eyes again, Nate saw that Emily had a frown on her face. "You all right?" he mouthed.

Emily nodded. But he could tell she was deep in thought. At last she spoke. "Do you think Stella has any relatives?"

Nate thought his mother looked relieved that Emily had brought up the topic.

"I don't know, but I've been thinking about it." Connie passed the platter of boiled dinner to Nate. "Stella lived in that beautiful old cottage for about forty years. I was here when she moved in. She was single at the time, but she married Edgar a couple of years after that."

"I saw some photos of her and Edgar at the house," Nate said.

"I didn't remember that Stella was ever married," said Emily.

"Edgar died ten years or so ago," said Dad Phillips as he took the platter from Nate and helped himself to the meat and vegetables. "It was before I moved here, but his grave is in the church cemetery, and Stella visited it often."

"You remember him, don't you, Nate?" his mother asked. "Edgar loved fishing. He was always out on the lake in summer."

Nate thought back to his junior high years. "Yeah. Seemed like he was always sunburned. He used to stand on the shore and throw saltine crackers at the ducks."

"Oh, I remember him!" said Emily. "He used to imitate Donald Duck and pretend the ducks on the lake were talking to him."

"Yes, that's him," said Connie.

"Yeah, I remember that bit," Nate said. "I've tried for years to learn the Donald Duck voice." He offered an exaggerated frown.

Emily rolled her eyes. "I for one am thankful you never picked it up."

"Edgar and Stella never had any children," said Connie. "I suppose she was all alone in the world."

"There should be an obituary in the *Journal*," said Emily. "Normally family members or the funeral directors write that. But I called the funeral home, and Stella hadn't left them any instructions. I guess I could do it, but I don't know that much about her."

"I can help you with it," said Connie. "A lot of the older people in town probably knew Stella better than I did, though. I could call some of her friends."

"Thanks. Felicia might be able to help, too. We should talk to her about it. In fact, I'm surprised she hasn't called me. She's usually so hot on the trail of a news story that she practically knows things before they happen."

Connie laughed.

Emily took a bite of her corned beef and chewed with an appreciative look on her face. "You've got to help me learn to cook like this, Mom. You're so good at it."

"Oh, thank you. I'd be happy to give you a lesson anytime."

Emily scrunched up her face and darted a glance at Nate. "I'm afraid Nate will suffer after we're married. He's used to your wonderful cooking. I can do the basics, but I never really took to it."

"I'm willing to be your guinea pig," Nate said. "Especially if you're learning to make pies." The others laughed, and he hated to turn the conversation back to more serious matters. "You know, Ward and I found Stella's address book this afternoon. Ward took it, along with some other papers. Maybe we could look in there for relatives."

"Good idea." Connie rose and refilled the water pitcher. "I'm pretty sure Edgar had a brother, at least. Of course, he wouldn't be a blood relative of Stella's, but his family would probably want to know she's passed away, and he might have an idea who else to contact."

"What about a funeral?" said Nate. "If she doesn't have any family, there won't be anyone to arrange for that, either."

"I could do a memorial service at the church," said his stepfather.

"That's a good idea, Jared." Connie refilled his water glass. "If Nate can get us Stella's address book, we can contact Edgar Lessard's brother about it. There may be others who would want to come for a memorial. It would be a shame for her to be buried without some kind of service." She let out a little sigh.

"I think it's sad she lived alone so long," said Emily. "I wish I'd thought to visit her before I had the idea of writing about her house."

"No sense getting lost in regrets," said Dad Phillips. "Once you start down that road, there's no end. We'll always wish we'd done more good than we have."

On Friday morning Nate walked into the Baxter marina and pulled a copy of that day's edition of the *Journal* off the stack on the counter. He laid a dollar bill down, and Allison Woods grinned at him.

"Good morning, Nate. I'm surprised you don't get your paper for free."

Nate chuckled. "I probably will, once Emily and I tie the knot. I don't mind paying for it, though. It's in my best interest to support the *Journal*."

"Say, we've got a hot prospect to buy our business and house." Allison handed him his change.

"That's great."

"Yeah, it looks like we might close by the end of the month. You know what that means."

Nate grinned. "It means you and Jonathan will both be here full-time when the summer rush starts."

"Right. Jon can handle the boat rentals and fuel and outboard motor parts, and I'll sell the food and souvenirs and take care of the bookkeeping."

"I'm glad it's working out for you guys." Nate's parents had owned the marina since before he was born, and he'd struggled over the decision to sell it. He and his mother had kept it going for a couple of years after his dad died. But now the time was right. His mother was married and settled in the parsonage, and Nate had begun his new career as a law officer. He and Emily would keep the Holmans' house next to the marina and live there, but within weeks the marina store and docks would belong to Jon and Allison.

"How's it going with the sheriff's department?" Allison asked.

"Great. I love it."

"I'm glad to hear that. Wouldn't want you to be having second thoughts."

Nate shook his head. "This is what I

always wanted to do. The idea of selling this place took a little getting used to, but now that Mom and I have made the decision, I can see that it's right for all of us."

An outboard motor started outside at the docks, and Jonathan came in the back door of the marina. "Okay, I sent that guy off in boat three. Hi, Nate."

"Wow, the ice just went out last week, and you're already renting boats," Nate said.

"Yeah, an early fisherman. But we're already doing quite a business. A man came a few days ago and wanted a boat for a couple of weeks," Allison said. "He's renting Henry Derbin's old cottage on Grand Cat."

"Anyone I know?" Nate asked.

"No, Bridget Kaplin is handling the cottage rental for Henry's granddaughter, Paulie. The renter is an older guy, from out of town."

"Seems early for summer people to arrive." Nate shook his head. "But then, Emily wants to move to the island for the summer this weekend, so I suppose that's what I'll be doing tomorrow — helping her move boxes out to the cottage. Well, you two have a great day."

"Thanks, Nate," Allison said.

He walked out into the parking lot. The

early May sunshine felt good on his shoulders. He leaned against his SUV and opened the paper, glanced at Emily's front page story on Stella Lessard's death, and turned to the obituary they had put together with help from his mother and Felicia Chadwick.

Stella P. Lessard, 65, a longtime resident of Baxter, died Thursday, May 5, at her home. She was married to the late Edgar B. Lessard for 28 years. She loved gardening and reading. A memorial service will be held at the Community Church, date to be announced.

Nate pursed his lips. It was so skimpy! But it was the best they could do on short notice. Maybe Emily could find out more before the next edition of the paper came out on Tuesday.

He skimmed through the longer article on page 1 then pulled out his cell phone and called Emily.

"Hi, Em? Just calling to say you did a good job with the story and the obit."

"Oh, thanks."

Nate held the paper up so he could look at the picture of Stella's cottage, which ran next to the story. "I'm glad Felicia let you put the pictures in and tell a little bit about Stella's house. It's a shame you didn't get to write your story before she died."

"I know," said Emily. "But it wasn't hard

news, anyway. It was more of a feature."

"Yes, but you like research and history. It was your kind of story." Nate looked up to see a gray Volvo gliding slowly down the street. The driver peered toward the marina and pulled into the parking lot. "I'd better get going," Nate said. He put his phone in his pocket and watched as a man in a suit got out of the Volvo and started walking toward him. He looked about forty-five years old, with short hair and metal-rimmed glasses. He was well groomed and stiff-backed.

"May I help you?" Nate asked.

"Could be." He eyed Nate's uniform. "I'm John Wolfe. I have a law practice in Aswontee."

Nate extended his hand. "Nate Holman, with the Penobscot County Sheriff's Department."

"Aha. You wouldn't know anything about Stella Lessard's death, would you?"

Nate looked into the lawyer's brown eyes, not sure how to respond. "Well, I was one of the first officers on the scene after her death was reported yesterday."

"Excellent." Wolfe smiled. "Mrs. Lessard came to me after her husband died and had me draw up a will for her. I have a copy of it on file at my office. The problem is, I may need to make the particulars public."

Nate studied him thoughtfully. "You mean you need to advertise in case there happens to be an heir?"

"Oh, there is an heir all right," said Wolfe. "At least, Mrs. Lessard indicated to me that there was. But locating the heir could be a problem."

"Hmm. You might want to talk to my fiancée, Emily Gray. She writes for the *Journal,* and she could help you publicize the information."

"That would be great," Wolfe said. "In fact, I drove over here with the idea of finding the *Journal* office and asking if they had any more information. How can I meet Miss Gray?"

"I'll take you over to the office now if you like," said Nate. "It'll only take a couple of minutes to get there."

"Oh, there's one other thing, Officer."

"Yes?" Nate paused.

"Mrs. Lessard also named an alternate heir, in case her preferred heir doesn't step forward."

That sounded a little weird to Nate, but he didn't want to sound ignorant, so he just waited, holding the lawyer's gaze, the way he'd been taught to do when he was taking a witness's statement.

Wolfe smiled. "I won't publicize this fact, but she stipulated that if the primary heir is not found within a year, her estate will go to someone else. Do you know a man named Cedar Sproul?"

Nate stared at him. His chuckle came out more like a snort. "Sure. You're telling me she left everything to Cedar?"

"Oh, no, not unless . . . You see, this Sproul apparently did a lot of work for Mrs. Lessard."

"Sure," Nate said. "He would cut wood for her and spade up her flower beds, things like that. But Cedar . . . uh . . ."

Wolfe smiled. "Just between you and me, she indicated that he might be one sandwich short of a picnic, so to speak. But she said he worked hard and was loyal to her. She wanted to leave him something. And she did. A thousand dollars. But if the other heir isn't found, the entire estate goes to him."

"To Cedar Sproul."

"That's right."

Nate shook his head slowly. "I can show you where Cedar lives if you want to talk to him. Are you going to tell him now?"

"I have to. But I'll also advise him to keep it quiet until we see how things are going to shake down. It's unlikely he'll inherit, and

I'll make him understand that."

"You mean you'll *try* to make him understand."

Wolfe's eyes narrowed. "Are you saying he's incapable of grasping the terms of the will?"

Nate held up both hands and smiled. "I'm sorry. Cedar's not brilliant, but he should be able to handle what you're telling me. Just . . . you might want to emphasize that you don't think he should tell anyone else. I mean, people can be mean, and someone like . . . oh, I don't know, say Edgar Lessard's family found out the estate might go to Stella's handyman, they might get upset, you know?"

"Yes." Wolfe pursed his lips for a moment. "Yes, I've seen things turn ugly when an inheritance was involved. I think it's best we don't publish that provision of the will, even though I need to announce my attempt to locate the true heir. Good advice, deputy."

John Wolfe and Emily sat opposite each other ten minutes later, with mugs of hot coffee on the desk between them. Emily jotted scraps of information in her notebook as they talked. Felicia sat at her desk across the room, typing laconically on her keyboard, but Emily was sure she was catching most of the conversation.

"So Mrs. Lessard had you write a new will after her husband died?" Emily asked.

"Yes. She and Edgar had wills before, leaving their complete estates to each other and appointing each other as representatives of the estates. They didn't indicate any other heirs at that time, although I suggested that they should. Stella came in a few years after Edgar died and changed hers."

Emily sipped her coffee, her mind racing with questions. "Mr. Wolfe, I'm not sure you can tell me this, but who is her executor now?"

He sighed. "Please don't publish this, but I am. It's not unusual for people to appoint their attorneys as their personal representatives, especially if they have no close relatives to act in that capacity."

"So it's up to you to distribute her estate."

"Correct. When I saw the *Baxter Journal* this morning and learned she was dead, I got out her file," Wolfe continued. "She didn't list a way to contact her heir."

"Isn't that unusual?"

"Very. But you see, she explained it to me at the time she changed the will. She didn't know at that time how to contact the heir. I urged her strongly to try to find out, but she never brought me more information, and so here we are. I thought perhaps you could help me."

"I'll do my best, Mr. Wolfe. What would you like me to do?"

"If you could publish an article about this, perhaps the heir would come forward." He ran his hand through his hair. "Maybe I should go to the *Bangor Daily.* It's a bigger paper, I know, but when I saw your story this morning, I decided to come here."

Emily's adrenaline surged. She felt a front-page story coming. "Our next edition comes out Tuesday. Is that soon enough for your purposes? Because we'd love to break the news in the *Journal.* Mrs. Lessard lived here for a long time, and I was supposed to interview her yesterday."

He arched his eyebrows. "Indeed?"

Emily considered how much to tell him and made a quick decision. "Mr. Wolfe, I discovered Stella's body when I went to her house for the interview."

"Oh, I'm sorry. That must have been a shock."

"Yes, it was. I want to help you find her heir. It'll let me feel like I've done something for Stella, even though I was too late yesterday."

Wolfe nodded. "Yes. I don't think it would hurt to delay seeing it in print for a couple of days. These things take time, and the estate will still be there."

Emily sat back, pleased with his decision. "You should be prepared for the news services and television stations to pick up the story when it's published, though. A search for a missing heir will draw a lot of attention."

"Good. That's what I want. I should be ready to handle all the inquiries by Tuesday."

"Fine." Emily bent over her notebook. "How do you want people to contact you with information?"

Wolfe gave her the phone number at his law office as well as an e-mail address.

"And who are you looking for? To whom did Stella Lessard decide to leave her estate?"

He smiled. "To a little girl."

Emily blinked and cocked her head to one side. "A little girl?"

"That's the way Stella remembered her. Of course, she'd be grown up now. The heir is her daughter, Lois."

3

On Saturday evening Nate lit the grill beneath the big pines in front of Emily's cottage. She pulled packages of meat and foil-wrapped vegetables from her cooler and handed them to him. He made a small adjustment to the burner controls and situated the steaks and foil packs on the grill rack.

"I've got to learn to do this," she said.

Nate laughed. "What's so hard about throwing food on the grill?"

Emily brushed her hair back. Instead of smiling, she eyed the grill as though it were a slightly scary opponent. "I can cook on a stove, but I always seem to burn anything I try to cook on that thing. And do you put the food right over the burner, or off to the side? It seems pretty complicated to me. Like those old algebra problems with all kinds of variables. You never could get a definitive answer, just a bunch of letters that have no meaning."

Nate shut the lid. "See this? It's your thermometer. If it says seven hundred degrees, don't put your food in. That would be like a seven-hundred-degree oven. Turn the burners down and let it cool off."

The color rose in Emily's cheeks, and he had the feeling it wasn't just from the heat radiating off the grill. She probably never thought to look at the temperature gauge on the front of the lid.

"Are you sure you'll trust me in the kitchen when we're married?" she asked.

"Oh, yeah. I've eaten your cooking before, and you're not nearly as bad as you make out to be." Nate fished in the cooler for two canned soft drinks and handed her one. He wasn't worried that he would starve after the wedding. He grabbed two plastic lawn chairs and carried them out onto the dock in front of Emily's cottage. She followed him and sat down, facing the lake.

"Pretty classy dock I've got, huh?" Her smile eased the tension.

"Best you can get these days." Nate had replaced the creaky old wooden dock for her last summer with a strong metal wharf frame and textured vinyl deck when she had thought she would sell the cottage.

A mile away, he could see the town of

Baxter, where a flag snapped in the breeze above the marina. Her summer cottage was the last in the row on Grand Cat, and off the marshy end of the island, Little Cat was just a quarter mile across the choppy water. In another month the boys' camp there would be swarming with small fry.

Nate took a deep swallow of his soda and leaned back with a sigh. "This is going to be great, Em."

"Living out here?"

"Yeah. I've always wanted to live on the island. You know that."

Her smile seemed content now, and he felt confident that the best part of their lives lay just a short stone's throw in the future. "You sure you'll be okay alone for now?"

"Absolutely. Raven's down at the camping center if I need help."

As far as Nate knew, their friend Raven Miller and a renter at the Derbin cottage on the far end of Grand Cat were the only others on the island so far.

"I think a couple of Raven's staff members are coming this week to help her set up the camp," Emily said, "and Truly Vigue told me she and Marvin are moving out next weekend."

Nate looked toward the Vigues' cottage, which was next to Emily's. "I hope they'll let Rocky come out this summer."

"Have you seen him lately?" she asked.

"Yeah, I stopped by yesterday. He and Clinker were outside. Rocky's trying to build a doghouse for that mutt, though why, I don't know. He lets Clinker sleep on the end of his bed." He smiled, remembering the little dog he and Emily had babysat for Rocky when he was in the hospital.

"Probably Rocky just needs a project to keep him busy, and he likes to do things for Clinker," she said.

"He's told me more than once that Clinker is the only one who loves him." Nate got up and went to turn the steaks over.

Emily set her diet cola in the holder on the arm of her chair and zipped her sweatshirt.

"Getting a little nippy," Nate agreed. "You want to eat inside when these are ready?"

"Maybe."

The idea of eating in her crowded kitchen didn't appeal much to him. The boxes he had helped her haul out in three boatloads from Felicia's house were mostly still piled in the kitchen and living room of the cottage. It would probably take her days to get everything unpacked and put away.

He looked up at the gray sky. He could forgive the unsettled weather of May because the next long winter was at least six months away. The lake was theirs for the summer. But the thought of Emily driving herself to the mainland in a small motorboat when the lake teemed with whitecaps was another thing.

He caught her glancing uneasily at the boat he had brought from her boathouse and moored for her at the side of the dock, closer to shore than his cabin cruiser.

"If it's windy in the morning, I'll come get you for church," he assured her. "Raven, too, if she wants to go."

"Thanks."

Emily didn't like relying on other people, Nate knew — even him. But being out on the big lake alone in foul weather would be dangerous for her. His inclusion of Raven in the invitation ought to give her a way to accept his offer without feeling incompetent.

"If it's really bad, don't come." Her blue eyes had a no-nonsense cast. "I don't want you performing heroics just to prove you can do it."

"Right. I'll run the orange flag up the marina flagpole if I'm not coming, just so you'll know."

Fifteen minutes later, he declared their dinner ready. Emily carried the platter up the path to the cottage, and Nate followed with the cooler. They cleared enough space on the pine kitchen table to spread out their dishes, and Emily found paper towels to use in place of napkins. Nate grasped her hand and asked a blessing for the food.

Emily opened her eyes and smiled at him. "First meal of the season on the island."

"Yeah. Many more to come."

They sat holding hands across the table and gazing into each other's eyes. A soft pattering of rain began on the roof. A big gust of wind shook the cottage, and the pattering became a deluge.

Nate's smile slid into a grimace. "I forgot to close the grill."

Emily jumped up. "We'd better get the chairs, too. Those light plastic things will blow into the lake." She flipped her hood up and ran to the door. Nate was close behind her. Rain sheeted off the porch roof.

"I've got an umbrella." Emily looked back toward the kitchen. "Somewhere in one of these boxes."

"Stay here," Nate said. "No sense us both getting wet." He dashed out into the rain. The path was already wet, and he slid, almost falling in the mud, but recovered and hurried down to the shore. He slammed the cover on the grill as he passed it. The wind lifted one of the chairs just as he reached the end of the dock, and it flew into his boat. Better than in the water. He grabbed the other one and dashed to the edge of the dock. As he clambered into his boat to reach the errant chair, holding the other by one leg so it wouldn't fly away in the wind, he couldn't help letting out a laugh. *Oh, yeah. Life with Emily is going to be one adventure after another.*

On Monday morning Nate came to the island for Emily at Felicia's request when she was an hour late for work. To her embarrassment, he found her sitting in her fourteen-foot aluminum boat in tears.

"I'm all right," she insisted.

"You sure?" He brought his cruiser in close to the other side of the dock.

"Yes, I'm sure. I just . . . oh, I might as well tell you. I flooded the stupid motor again."

"Come on. I'll take you over. It's still choppy, anyway."

"Then someone will have to bring me back later."

"It's okay. I'll tow your boat. Come on."

She sighed and gathered her totebag and laptop case and climbed onto the dock and into his boat while he pulled her smaller craft around and tied the painter to the stern of his cabin cruiser.

That afternoon Nate gave her an hour's patient instruction before he left to join Ward for their afternoon patrolling. Emily took herself home to the island determined to learn to run the outboard and gain the freedom that would bring. Driver's ed had been nowhere near as difficult as this.

On Tuesday morning the weather had calmed, and she managed to start the outboard motor and arrive at the *Journal* office on time.

"Hey, girl!" Felicia grinned as she entered the office. "Making friends with that boat, are you?"

"We're bosom buddies." Emily laid her bundles on her desk and nodded at Charlie Benton, who was the *Journal*'s entire advertising department. "Morning, Charlie."

"We've already had six calls about your article." Felicia rose, grinning, and held out a slip of paper. "A reporter from Channel 5 in Bangor called. He's going to try to snag an interview with Wolfe, but he hasn't made contact with him yet, and he wanted to check in with you on some details about the will."

"He'd better talk to Mr. Wolfe," Emily said. "Who else called?"

"People from here in town and Aswontee,

wanting to know how much money Stella left and trying to tell me she never had any kids."

Emily raised her eyebrows and scanned the list. "I guess we learned differently about that, didn't we?"

"Yeah," Felicia said. "Monty Capper asked if we were going to run a correction on Friday's story, where you said she had no children. I told him I thought today's piece constituted a correction."

"You live and learn," Charlie said, not looking up from the ad layout he had spread out on his desk. "Felicia, I'll be on the road most of the day, collecting ad copy. And I want to try that new computer place in Aswontee again and see if I can convince them to advertise."

"Hey, try the funeral home, too." Felicia's hazel eyes glittered.

"They got a free mention Friday and today," Charlie said. "I doubt they'll pay for an ad when they're getting it for nothing."

"Besides," Emily pointed out, "they're the only funeral parlor in the area. Do they really need to advertise?"

Felicia scowled at them. "We should be able to find a way to make them think they do."

"I like the way you think, lady." Charlie

began to stack his papers.

The phone on Emily's desk rang, and she picked up the receiver.

"*Baxter Journal.*"

"Hello," said a timid female voice. "I'm calling about that missing heir story."

"How may I help you?" Emily asked.

"The paper said that if that woman's daughter isn't found in one year, the estate will go to somebody else."

"That's correct."

"Who?"

"Mrs. Lessard's attorney did not reveal that information. The will is a confidential document, but he made part of it public in an effort to find the heir."

"So I guess you won't tell me how much the estate is worth, either."

Nervy. Emily made a face at Felicia, who made no attempt to hide the fact that she was listening. "Actually, I don't know the estate's value. We did publish the attorney's address and telephone number. I suggest you call Mr. Wolfe with your questions."

When she had hung up, Emily detailed the conversation to Felicia.

Her friend's eyes widened. "Do you think that could have been Stella's daughter on the phone?"

Emily shook her head slowly. "Doubtful.

She sounded awfully young. Stella's daughter has to be over forty, Mr. Wolfe said. And she has to show up with documentation of her identity if she hopes to get her hands on the estate."

Felicia nodded. "The TV stations will broadcast it tonight, and I'm betting the AP will pick up your story. This may get nationwide attention. We'll probably get all kinds of crackpots and con artists calling, hoping they can horn in on the inheritance."

Emily opened her laptop. "I'm not going to think about that right now. I'm going to start working on the advance story for the fishing derby. Memorial Day is just a few weeks away, and Jeff Lewis gave me a list of prizes and a copy of the rules."

"Great. We'll run it Friday." Felicia turned back to her work.

Emily pulled her folder on the fishing derby from her tote bag and opened a new computer file, but her thoughts kept returning to the Edwardian cottage in the woods. If Stella's daughter was found, would she want to live in the house? And why had no one in Baxter ever known about Lois? Even Edgar Lessard's brother claimed he had no knowledge of her. Edgar had never mentioned a stepdaughter to him. Why had Stella hidden the fact that she'd had a daughter before she married Edgar? There was a bigger story there, Emily was sure.

She sighed and began typing up the rules for the fishing derby.

4

"One vanilla chai latte, and a whole grain English muffin," said Felicia on Thursday morning, setting a Styrofoam cup and small paper bag on Emily's desk. "Get it while it's hot."

"Thanks." Emily looked up from her computer. "Have you tried the English muffins yet? These things are addictive."

"Nope. You know me. I take my coffee and I'm good to go."

"Hey." Charlie cleared his throat.

"Did you want something?" Felicia asked sarcastically.

"Where's my double espresso and chocolate cream doughnut?"

"I'd have to go to Aswontee for that," said Felicia. "Besides, you were late coming in today, and I don't remember you being present when I took orders." She wrinkled her brow. "Boy, I'm glad we don't have a doughnut shop in Baxter. I'd inflate!"

"Not if we had a gym, too," said Emily. "Sometimes I have to admit I miss the city."

"Maybe I'll open a Dunkin' Donuts," said Charlie. "After we go to a daily, and I'm rich."

The girls laughed.

Emily took a sip of her latte. She heard a motor outside, and then a car door slammed. "I wonder who that is?"

"No idea," Felicia said.

"My personal doughnut delivery guy?" Charlie stretched his arms up over his head and yawned.

Felicia took a long drink of coffee. "Oh, that's good. Mm, mm."

A moment later the door swung open and a young woman entered the office. "Excuse me? Is this the office of the *Baxter Journal*?"

Emily stared at her, caught off guard by her appearance.

"Yes, ma'am," said Felicia. "How can I help you?"

The young woman was slender — almost too thin — with her spindly legs displayed in black jeans. Her short jet black hair was spiked all around.

Emily took inventory of her piercings and saw a black stud eyebrow ring, a tiny silver lip ring, and multiple pairs of earrings. A tattoo of a green and black snake slithered around her left wrist, and a curved row of sinister-looking black flowers was tattooed across her collarbone, just above the neckline of her purple-and-gray camouflage T-shirt. Her eyes were heavily outlined, and her lashes were thick with mascara. Or were they eyelash extensions? Emily wondered. She had heard of such things but never knew anyone who wore them.

"I'm Jeanette Williams." The young woman paused, as if expecting them to recognize the name.

"And I'm Felicia Chadwick." Felicia looked slightly perturbed.

"I'm Emily Gray." Emily tried not to stare. "What can we do for you?"

"Oh, sorry. I heard about Stella Lessard's recent death. Well, I'm her granddaughter."

"Wow!" Felicia set her coffee cup down. "First a daughter, now a granddaughter. I wonder if all my relatives would come visit me if I died?"

Behind them Charlie tried to disguise a laugh by coughing.

"Sorry, Jeanette," said Felicia quickly. "I didn't mean to be disrespectful. I'm sorry about your grandmother. She was a nice lady."

"Call me Jette. It's okay. I never really knew my grandmother. My mom was her daughter from her first marriage."

"Welcome." Emily stood and extended her hand. "I always assumed Stella had only been married once. I wish we'd known. We could have mentioned you and your mother in the obituary."

"Hmm." Jette looked her over critically. "My mom's gone, too."

"I'm so sorry," said Emily. "My dad died when I was young. I know it's rough."

"Yeah. But you get on with it."

There was an awkward silence.

"How about seeing my grandmother's house?" Jette said at last.

Emily looked over at Felicia. "Mind if I step out to show her?"

"Fine by me. But don't forget to come back. It gets lonely in here when you go gallivanting all over the place. Especially when Charlie starts rocking in his chair and knitting something that isn't there."

Jette laughed.

Emily thought she had a pretty smile, if you could get past the gleaming lip ring.

"Ah, ha, very funny," said Charlie.

"I've got some boxes and stuff in the car," said Jette as they left the office. "It will be great to have a hand unpacking."

"Oh. Were you planning to move into the house?" Emily was pretty sure the police wouldn't allow that. The results of the autopsy weren't even in, as far as she knew.

"Yeah, I figured on it." Jette looked Emily straight in the eye. "Is that a problem? I mean, I am her granddaughter, and since Mom's dead, I'm technically Grandma's heir, right?"

"Well, I'm not sure," said Emily. "I would think so, but Mrs. Lessard's attorney can tell you about that." She got the feeling Jette would put up a fight if she tried to stop her from taking possession of the house. But she also knew from experience that the police would be very unhappy with her if she let someone move in on their territory. And the keys to the house were being held by the sheriff's department and John Wolfe, according to Nate.

"So, what's the problem?" Jette rested her hand on her hip, standing next to her car.

Emily thought carefully. "I think we'd better wait and see what the police and the attorney say. The police haven't finished their investigation yet. The house is locked up, and you won't be able to go in unless they say you can."

"Okay, I get you. Sounds fair. Where can I hang my hat until they're done with their yellow tape thing?"

"There's a bed-and-breakfast not far from here."

Jette thought, jiggling her head up and down as if in time to some imaginary music. "Sounds good. Is it like the Stafford Inn from the *Newhart* show?"

Emily laughed. "Stratford. A lot smaller. But just as friendly."

"Hopefully just as weird," said Jette. "Okay, I'd still like to see the house. Hop in, newspaper girl."

Emily wasn't sure why, but she thought Jette might make a good friend despite her strange appearance. She liked the young woman's carefree spirit. She climbed into the car and directed Jette on how to get to Stella's house.

"I've never been this far north," Jette said as she drove. "It's kind of pretty up here in the boondocks."

Emily smiled. "I grew up here. I went away to college and then got a job at a newspaper in Connecticut. But I came back last year, and I'm so glad I did."

"Does everybody know everybody?" Jette asked. "Like in Mayflower?"

"Mayflower?" Emily asked quizzically.

"From the *Andy Griffith Show.* Sorry, I spend too many evenings watching TV Land. I need a life."

"Oh, Mayberry!"

"Yeah, that's it."

Emily laughed. "I guess so. It is a very small town."

"Hey, but that's cool."

"Where are you from?" Emily asked.

"Dover, New Hampshire. It took me, like, five hours to drive up here. Of course, I stopped once for coffee."

"Turn left up ahead," Emily said.

Jette reached for her turn signal. "I kind of wish I'd been up to see my grandmother before she died. It would have been nice to connect with my roots. Find out if I have any hick tendencies buried underneath all this city."

Emily wondered what Jette would have been like as a kid. Maybe they would have played together if she'd come to see her grandmother in the summers. "Why didn't your mom ever bring you here?"

"Dunno," said Jette. "She didn't really have much use for her mother and stepdad, I guess. It was all kind of complicated. And after my mom died of breast cancer a couple of years ago, I sort of forgot I had roots up here. I wish I had come up, though. Maybe Grandma and I would have hit it off. So now I'll never know. I've got nobody. It gets kind of lonely, you know?"

Emily tried to think of what to say. She was afraid Jette would be closed to hearing about God, but then she chided herself for assuming something she didn't know. "Yes. I miss my father," she said softly, "but God is always there."

Jette concentrated on the road. She didn't look at Emily when she said, "Yeah, I suppose He is. Somewhere or other."

"Here we are." Emily pointed to the picturesque little house nestled in a clearing in the woods.

"Looks like a Three-Bears cottage."

As Jette pulled into the driveway, Nate's police cruiser turned in behind her.

"Uh-oh," said Jette, eyeing the car. "I suppose I broke some boondocks driving law."

"That's my fiancé." Emily giggled in spite of herself. "He was going to meet me for lunch. Felicia probably told him I was out here."

"That's a relief."

They got out of the car and walked over to meet Nate.

"Nate, this is Jeanette Williams," said Emily. "Stella's granddaughter."

"Hi, Jeanette." Nate didn't bat an eyelash at her flamboyant makeup and accessories. Felicia must have warned him.

Jette was staring at the house. "Hmm? Oh,

hi. Call me Jette. This is a great house. I love it." She started walking toward the porch.

"She came into the *Journal* office a few minutes ago and introduced herself," Emily said to Nate. "No warning."

"That's interesting." Nate frowned. "Did she say anything about Lois?"

"She said her mother died, and that she was Stella's daughter from her first marriage. I assume that's the Lois in the will. And, Nate, she thought she could move into the house."

"Really? I hope you told her otherwise."

"I tried not to be forceful. I said the police probably weren't done with the investigation, and I told her she could stay at the Heron's Nest."

"Okay, that's good. So, do you want to go to the Lumberjack?"

"We don't have to eat out all the time."

"But I want french fries." Nate grinned sheepishly.

Emily shook her head. "You're funny. Okay, that's fine with me."

Nate turned to watch Jette as she climbed the steps to the house. "She's kind of weird-looking, with her hair sticking out all over."

Emily smiled. "Yes, she is. But she seems nice enough. Should we ask her if she wants to come with us for lunch?"

"Nah," said Nate. "But we can show her how to get to the bed-and-breakfast when she's done poking around. And she should probably talk to Mr. Wolfe as soon as possible."

Emily and Nate waited as Jette looked around the porch. The yellow police line tape was still fixed across the door, but she reached past it and tried the knob.

"Nervy, isn't she?" Nate whispered. "She can't get in until she proves who she is to the lawyer."

Jette peered inside windows and bent over the porch railing to look at the flower beds. A few moments later, she turned and walked slowly to the porch steps, descended them, and sauntered down the path.

"All set?" Emily asked. "I'll ride over to the Heron's Nest with you." She climbed into the car again, and Jette took the wheel. They drove to the Heron's Nest with Nate following in his cruiser. Nate offered to help carry her things inside, although Emily knew he would much rather be diving into his burger and fries at the Lumberjack. At last they left Jette to settle into her room and headed to the restaurant for lunch.

Later that afternoon, Nate drove east on

the Aswontee Road to meet Ward. The sun beat down on the new foliage. He wished he were out on the lake.

A car zoomed around the corner ahead and rushed toward him. Nate activated the radar. Seventy-four miles per hour. He turned on his siren, whipped the car around, and started pursuit with the lights flashing. Not the same rush as driving a boat, but not bad, either.

A few seconds later, the driver of the light blue sedan pulled over without attempting to elude him. Nate parked on the shoulder behind the car. After a quick call to the dispatcher, he got out of his cruiser. He stepped toward the driver's door, and the woman inside rolled down her window.

"Howdy. Do you know why I stopped you?" Nate asked.

The young woman looked up at him. She had long, wavy brown hair and wore no makeup. She looked like she might be in her late teens. "No," she said with wide-eyed innocence.

"I clocked you on my radar at seventy-four miles an hour," Nate said, rather disgusted. Why did she bother to deny it? "Do you know what the speed limit is on this road?"

"You're kidding me. I couldn't have been

going more than sixty."

"The speed limit is fifty-five on this stretch of road. I need to see your license and registration."

The woman let out an exasperated sigh. "This is ridiculous." She took her brown leather purse from the passenger seat and dug around until she found her driver's license. "Here," she said acidly, handing it to Nate.

Nate took the license and looked at it. When he saw the name, he squinted and looked again. *That's strange,* he thought. She looked nothing like the young woman Emily had just introduced him to. And yet the name on the license was Jeanette Williams.

5

"I'm just going to give you a warning, Miss Williams." Nate checked off "excessive speed" and handed her the warning and her documents. They looked legit, and he had run them on the computer in the patrol car. Jeanette Williams appeared to be who she said she was. Which made him wonder seriously about the Goth girl he and Emily had parked at the Heron's Nest two hours ago. "Are you heading for Baxter?"

"Yes. How did you know?"

He shrugged. "There's not much else out here."

"Oh. Well, do you know if there's a hotel in town?"

Nate shook his head. "There's a bed-and-breakfast. The Heron's Nest. When you come into town, you'll pass the marina on your left. Keep going a couple hundred yards, and you'll see the B and B on the right."

"Thank you."

"And watch your speed, ma'am."

"I will, Officer."

He watched thoughtfully as she pulled into the traffic lane and drove at a modest pace toward Blue Heron Lake. Something told him he'd better cruise on over to the Heron's Nest.

When he entered the lobby and pulled off his sunglasses, Rita Eliot was passing the newcomer a pen so she could register. As Jeanette Williams of the blue car caught sight of him, a flicker of anxiety crossed her face.

"Is there a problem, Officer?"

"No," Nate said. "I'm here to see another one of the guests." He looked at Rita, who owned the B and B with her husband. "You know, the one Emily and I brought over this afternoon."

"Oh, you mean Miss Williams," Rita said with a smile. "Give me a minute, Nate, and I'll tell her you're here."

"Miss Williams?" Jeanette Williams stared at him for a second then turned to Rita. "There's another Miss Williams staying here?"

Rita looked down at the registration card Jeanette had just completed. "Oh, my, that's odd."

"Isn't it?" Nate managed a smile.

Rita turned and opened a file box. She took out another card, held it next to Jeanette's, and frowned. "I don't know what to say, Nate. I was so glad you'd brought me a guest so early in the season."

"Maybe you could just inform the other Miss Williams that I'd like to talk to her," he suggested.

"Certainly." Rita picked up her telephone and turned her back.

Jeanette scowled at Nate. "Officer, would you mind explaining to me what's going on here?"

"You came about the inheritance, didn't you?" Nate asked. "Stella Lessard's estate."

"Well, yes, but how did you know? I only learned a couple of days ago that my grandmother had died, and I took time off work to come up here and speak to the attorney about it."

"You've spoken to Mrs. Lessard's attorney, then?"

"I stopped by his office on my way here."

Nate felt a bit of relief at that news. "Good. Mr. Wolfe is reviewing your claim, then."

Her gaze fell. "Actually, he was out and I spoke with his secretary. I'll be meeting with Mr. Wolfe tomorrow morning at nine

64

o'clock. I came on to Baxter hoping to see the house where my grandmother lived and perhaps meet some of her neighbors."

"That's fine," Nate said. "But you ought to know that you aren't the only person putting in a claim on the estate."

"What do you —"

She broke off as Jette came bouncing down the stairs into the lobby.

"Hey there, Nate! How's Officer Friendly doing?" Jette grinned at him, paying no attention to Jeanette.

Nate cleared his throat and determined to keep a professional demeanor. Jeanette was glaring daggers at Jette, and he had a feeling it might have been wiser to speak to the spike-haired girl in private. "I'm fine, Miss Williams —"

"Hey, we're on a first-name basis, aren't we? You lugged all my junk in for me, remember?"

"Uh, yeah." Nate shot a glance at Jeanette, whose pupils were huge. Her face had gone a deep red.

"Is *that* the one?"

Nate looked from Jette, with her attention-demanding getup, to Jeanette, a natural-look girl from next door or the house next to that. "Uh, ladies, I guess I should introduce you. Jette Williams, this is Jeanette Williams.

And Jeanette —"

"What?" Jette stared at Jeanette. "Who do you think you are, using my name?"

"Me?" Jeanette's jaw dropped and she looked around at Rita and Nate, as though expecting them to leap to her defense. "Me using *your* name?"

"That's right. Jeanette is my given name. Jette is a nickname."

Jeanette's mouth closed and her eyes narrowed as she took her opponent's measure. "Well, Jeanette Williams is my *legal* name. I don't know where you get off trying to use it, honey, but if you think you can get your freaky black claws on my grandmother's estate, there's a lawyer down the road who'll set you straight."

Jette slapped her own cheek in mock horror, with her black-polished fingernails like jewels against her white skin. "Oh! You must be talking about John Wolfe, the attorney who's meeting with me at ten tomorrow morning about my grandmother's estate. I'm really scared."

"You little —"

Nate jumped between them, afraid Jeanette would launch herself against Jette any second. He felt like slapping them both. Instead, he held up his hands.

"Look, ladies, there's obviously some

mistake here. Uh, I don't suppose you two have ever met? Cousins, maybe?"

Jette giggled. "Oh, right. Identical cousins, like *The Patty Duke Show*? Only we don't look alike, genius."

Rita spoke up hesitantly. "Well, it's kind of hard to tell." She pointed at Jeanette. "I mean, *she* could be the one who likes opera, but I don't know about . . ."

Nate almost laughed, but she had a point. Who knew what was beneath Jette's hair gel, makeup, and hardware?

"I don't have any cousins on my . . ." Jeanette looked away.

"Me, neither. Not on Mom's side." Jette stepped down off the bottom step of the stairway and around Nate. She approached Jeanette, peering closely at her. "As to Dad, well, who knows, since he hasn't been around for years and years."

"Okay," Nate said, perhaps a little louder than was necessary. "We've established that you both claim to be heirs to the Lessard estate, and that you have the same name, although you say you've never met."

"I've never seen her before in my life." Jeanette crossed her arms and glared at Jette.

"Well, if I ever saw you before, sweet pea, I didn't find any reason to remember the occasion." Jette returned her hard look, and with the heavy eyeliner and thick lashes, she easily won the scary stare contest.

Jeanette looked away first and whirled toward the counter. "I'm sorry, but I can't stay here."

"Oh." Rita looked over at Nate then back at Jeanette. "Are you sure? This could be interesting."

"I'm sure. If you could please tear up that card, I'll find another place to stay. I can't be in the same building with that impostor."

Rita's mouth worked for an instant, but nothing came out, and her face crumpled into a dithery smile.

Jette stepped forward. "I'm the impostor, am I? Well, guess what? I got here first, and I've got the birth certificate to prove I am who I say I am. If you want to hit the road, that's your choice. I'm certainly not going anywhere."

"Uh, Miss . . . uh . . . Jette, take it easy." Nate tried to smile, but he was about smiled out for the day. "It sounds as though you're both planning to consult Mr. Wolfe tomorrow. I'm sure he can straighten this out. In the meantime, Miss Will— uh, Jeanette, we don't have another hotel in town."

"There's Lakeview Lodge," Rita piped up.

Nate threw her a glance of gratitude. "Great idea. Could you please call Jeff and see if he has a room Miss Williams — *this* Miss Williams — could rent?"

"How far away is it?" Jeanette asked.

"Not that far."

"Because I don't want to be stuck out in the woods somewhere while this impostor is in town."

"Well, it's actually a little closer than this to your grand— I mean, to Stella Lessard's house." Nate wished more than anything that he hadn't been on duty this afternoon. *Why, oh why did I have to go out the Aswontee Road today?*

Rita made a quick call and told Jeanette pleasantly, "There now, dear. They have a nice room for you at the lodge. And they've just remodeled there. I'm sure you'll like it."

"Thank you. How do I get there?"

Nate hesitated, but he figured he'd better treat both claimants equally, or he'd never hear the end of it. "If you want to follow my patrol car, ma'am, I'll lead you over there. It's only a couple of miles."

Jeanette threw a final glare at Jette and headed for the door. Nate nodded at Rita and followed.

"Hey, Boy Scout," Jette called after him.

Nate turned in the doorway and arched his eyebrows.

"If any more Jeanette Williamses show up in this burg, give me the high sign, will ya?"

Half an hour later, Nate threw the door to the *Journal*'s office open so hard it hit the wall. Felicia and Emily both jumped from their chairs.

"Oh, Nate, you scared me." Emily sat down again. "What's up?"

"You are not going to believe it."

"Try me."

"Yeah, we're in the news biz, after all," Felicia drawled.

"This is weirder than anything you've ever printed before."

"Weirder than lobster ice cream at the dairy bar?" Felicia asked. "That's going to be their new flavor this summer."

"Much weirder." Nate crossed the room, flopped into Charlie's empty chair, and looked across at Emily, shaking his head. "You know your little friend, Jette?"

Emily glanced at Felicia. "Well, I'm not so sure she's a friend on such short acquaintance, but yes, I know who you mean."

"Well, there's two of them."

"Two of what?" Emily asked.

"There's another girl calling herself

Jeanette Williams and trying to get Stella Lessard's money."

Felicia gaped at him then grinned. "Wowzer."

"You're right," Emily said. "That beats all for weirdness. It's even weirder than finding Raven Miller's class ring in an old grave."

"Or your treasure hunt out at the lodge," Felicia added.

Emily caught the spirit and laughed. "Or Rocky Vigue breaking through the ice."

Nate sat up and slapped Charlie's desk. "I'm telling you, this is weirder than any of that. It was a regular catfight. You should have seen them. I was afraid Jette would rip into Jeanette with those black nails of hers. And Jeanette, well, she's a piece of work. She looks sweet and innocent, but you don't want to mess with her, I'll tell you."

"Nate, this is a huge story. You need to tell us everything." Felicia set her tape recorder on her desktop and turned it on.

"Better yet, we need to interview the two girls." Emily grabbed a notebook and jumped up. "Felicia, call the printer. Tell him we'll deliver our front page late, and we'll have an extra large run for tomorrow's paper. We're going to sell out this edition." She ran for the door but stopped and turned when she reached it. "Are they both at the

Heron's Nest?"

Nate let out a guffaw. "No, this town ain't big enough for the both of them. I took the second one out to the lodge."

"Right. Good move. Say, we'd better get pictures of them both." Emily strode back to her desk and opened the lower drawer.

Nate sat up straight in his chair. "Hold on, Em. You know, when Jette came in here this morning and told you who she was, did she show you any identification?"

Emily started to speak then swallowed and glanced over at Felicia, but the editor was just sitting there, listening and smiling.

"Well, no."

"Exactly. We all accepted that she was who she claimed to be. But we have no proof that Jette is really Stella's granddaughter. And now this other young woman comes along with *the same name.* I saw her driver's license, and I'm telling you, it's freaky."

"One of them's lying." Felicia nodded with certainty.

"Gotta be," Nate agreed.

Emily sat down slowly. "My investigative reporting skills are getting rusty. You're absolutely right about Jette. I never once asked her for identification. I figured that was up to the lawyer. I sort of thought we'd wait until John Wolfe made an announcement that the heir had been found. But now . . ." She let out a puff of a breath.

"I believed her," Felicia agreed. "That Jette girl seems like a lot of fun. She's young and crazy, but she's likable."

"Yes," Emily said. "And her story touched me. She said her mother died of breast cancer. What if it's all a lie? I mean, anyone could come here and claim to be Stella's daughter Lois or one of Lois's children." She stared at Felicia. "There could be a dozen phony heirs before this estate is closed."

Nate nodded. "Maybe the first person you should talk to is John Wolfe."

"Well, what about you?" Felicia asked him. "If one or both of these so-called heirs is lying, shouldn't you be pressing some fraud charges?"

Nate gritted his teeth and considered whether he had, after all, done his duty.

Emily said, "Nate, honey, maybe you should call the sheriff and tell him about this. You know, before it gets any more complicated."

"Good idea."

"You can use our phone if you want," Felicia said.

Nate chuckled. "So you can listen? No, thanks."

"Okay, but you have to let us know the official response to these developments." Felicia turned off the tape recorder with a frown.

Emily followed him out the door. "I'm going to try to call John Wolfe, like you said. And I think Felicia and I *should* interview the two girls. I mean, this is big, Nate. Really big. If we wait, the TV crew will be here from Bangor, breaking our story."

He stooped and kissed her lightly. "You do what you've gotta do, babe. I don't think a crime has been committed. Not yet. But it could be that one of those girls is impersonating the other and contemplating fraud. If that's so, then the law will have to step in. I'll see what the sheriff says, but as far as I can tell, nobody's crossed the line yet."

"Unless one of them has a fake driver's license or something like that."

"Right." Nate climbed into his official car and drove up to the town office at the top of the knoll, where the best reception for cell phone service was to be found in Baxter, and called his boss.

"That's downright strange," the sheriff said, when Nate had told his story.

"Yes, sir. What do you think I should do now?"

"Well, like you say, if nobody's done anything . . ."

"I should have ticketed the one I stopped for speeding."

"Now that was a judgment call," the sheriff said. "Next time, maybe you'll do that. But you say the lawyer is going to look at their documentation?"

"Yes, sir. They have to present proof of their identity in order to claim the estate."

"Mm-hmm. Well, why don't you just touch base with him and arrange for a little one-on-one time tomorrow, after he's interviewed these young ladies? Let him know we want to be kept up-to-date on what happens."

Nate exhaled in relief. "I'll do that, sir."

"Good. And in the meantime, it would probably be smart for you to contact officials in the girls' hometowns. Maybe you can find out which one is lying."

6

Emily moored her boat at Nate's dock the next morning. She yawned as she looped the end of the painter over a post and grabbed the ladder.

"Hey, sleepyhead!" Nate grinned as he walked out onto the dock to meet her. "You're late getting to work this morning."

"Felicia and I were up till all hours changing the pages for today's paper." She gladly accepted his offer of a hand as she climbed onto the dock. "How are you doing?"

"Good." He bent to kiss her. "Even better now."

Emily lingered for another kiss. "You're in uniform early."

"Yeah, I'm going into Aswontee on official business." He reached for her laptop case and carried it for her. "I have an appointment with John Wolfe at eleven."

"After both Williams girls see him."

"That's the general idea. Have you had

breakfast?" He stopped as they came to the back door of his house.

"No, I'll have coffee at the office."

"I've got muffins. Mom brought them over last night."

She let her posture wilt. "Ooh, you know I can't resist your mom's muffins."

He laughed and opened the back kitchen door for her. A few minutes later they sat at the table together with coffee and plenty of blueberry muffins.

"These are berries she froze last summer," Nate said.

Emily slathered on the margarine. "This is so worth being late to work. Don't tell Felicia, though. Of course, I'm counting on her sleeping late, too. Did you find out anything yesterday?"

"Not really. I spent all afternoon on the phone after I left you. As far as I can tell, both Jeanette Williamses appear to have legitimate backgrounds."

"But . . . they can't both be telling the truth."

He shrugged. "That's why I'll be talking to Mr. Wolfe."

"Yeah. When I called him yesterday, he had no idea what was going on. He said he'd be meticulous about making them prove their identity, though. Felicia interviewed Jette last night, and I went to the lodge and interviewed Jeanette. We didn't find any holes in their stories, either."

When she'd finished her muffin, Emily looked longingly at the plate. "Nope. I'm not having seconds. I've got to fit in my wedding dress."

Nate scowled at her. "What's this? You look great."

She pushed her chair back. "Thanks, but I've indulged in far too much of your mom's good cooking lately."

"If you say so. I'll walk over to the office with you."

They stepped outside into the sunshine. Emily glanced toward the marina. "Well, look at that."

Jeanette exited the marina store, the door of which was held open for her by their chunky friend, Rocky Vigue. Each carried a bulging sack with the marina's logo on it, and Rocky's small dog, Clinker, pranced beside his master.

"Hey, Rocky," Nate called.

"Hi, Nate!" Rocky glanced toward Jeanette, beaming.

"Good morning, Miss Williams," Nate added. "I believe you've met my fiancée, Emily Gray."

"Yes. Nice day." Jeanette nodded briefly

and put her sack into her blue sedan. She turned and took the second bag from Rocky. "Thanks again."

"No trouble," Rocky said. "Listen, if you'd like someone to show you around town, I'd love to be the one."

"Thank you, but no," Jeanette replied. "I have an appointment." She got into the car and drove away.

Rocky stood on the pavement watching. His shoulders drooped as her car drove out of sight.

"We'll see you later, Rocky," Emily called.

Nate touched her arm. "Hey, do you mind if I don't walk over with you? Rocky looks like he could use a little cheering up."

Emily smiled. *I'm marrying the most tenderhearted man in Maine.* "Yeah, that's a good thought. I'll call you later." She squeezed his hand then took her laptop case from him and hurried to the *Journal* office.

To her surprise, Felicia was just unlocking the door.

"Good morning!" Emily hurried down the sidewalk.

"If you say so."

"Oh, someone's grouchy."

Felicia winced. "Just put the coffee on, would you?" The phone was ringing when she opened the door, and she dived for it.

"Oh, hello, Mr. Wilding. Yes, it's developing into a fascinating story."

Emily recognized the name of the news producer from one of the Bangor television stations. Good thing Felicia had answered the phone. She sat down and plunged into her assignments for Tuesday's paper. They kept her busy for an hour, between phone interruptions. She still had to write the most important story for the next edition. The update on the Lessard estate would be written Monday afternoon to be sure they got the very latest information, but she could do some background work now.

She took out her notes from the day before. Jeanette Williams had stated she worked at a daycare center in Harpswell. Jette said she waitressed at a seafood restaurant in Dover, New Hampshire. Emily was determined to prove whether or not those simple claims were true.

Around noon, Nate called her and asked her to meet him at the marina house for lunch. By the time he arrived, Emily had fixed eggs and sausage to go with the rest of Connie's muffins.

"Finding your way around your future kitchen, I see," Nate said with a smile as he entered.

"I figure it's in my best interest." She

melted into his arms for a kiss then turned to take up the food. "Sit right down while it's hot. I didn't burn anything."

He asked the blessing and picked up his fork. "Em, I talked to John Wolfe."

"What did he say? Because I tried my best to poke holes in those girls' stories, and I couldn't do it. I found both their employers after some sleuthing and got telephone testimonials. They hold the jobs they claim to, under the names they gave us. I felt so guilty afterward that I called them both and invited them to church."

Nate smiled. "That's nice, but you shouldn't feel guilty. Mr. Wolfe didn't have much better luck than you did. I guess I've got to interview them again and ask more questions. Wolfe said that if one is an impostor, she's done a very good job of building her identity and covering her tracks for a nineteen-year-old."

Nate knocked on the door to Jette's room.

"One second!" came a muffled reply. "Wet fingernails!"

Nate shook his head. He had seen Emily wear nail polish on only one or two occasions, and it had been pale pink. He was glad she didn't spend a lot of time fussing about her fingernails.

At last Jette cracked the door open. "Oh, it's you, Nate."

"Have you got a minute to come down to the lobby?" Nate asked. "I'd like to ask you some more questions."

"Okay. Anything to figure out who that girl thinks she is." Jette looked down at her hands. "Right, these are nearly set."

They headed down to the lobby, where Nate invited her to sit down in the cozy living room area. Jette took one of the dark brown plush armchairs and crossed her legs Indian style on the cushion. "So, what's up?" She smiled brightly, as though she enjoyed the prospect of being interviewed by a cop.

"You may know that I've spoken to Stella's lawyer," said Nate.

"I figured." Jette examined her nails critically. They glittered like polished onyx. "I've already told him my whole life story, which he no doubt communicated to you. What else do you need to know?"

Nate knew she was right. But he hoped maybe she could tell him something the lawyer had neglected to ask or something she hadn't thought was important. "Tell me about your childhood. Who did you live with while you grew up?"

"I lived with my mom pretty much," said Jette.

"Pretty much?"

"The story goes, my dad disappeared when I was a baby. So, I guess he was there for a while, but I don't remember him at all. And I've had no contact with him. Mom never wanted to talk about him. I figure he's a real jerk."

Nate nodded. "So, your mom never got money from him to help with your support or anything like that?"

"Trust me, I'd have known. We were flat broke all the time. When Mom got sick and couldn't work, I started waitressing."

"What happened when your mom died?"

"I got my own place," said Jette. "I've been on my own for two years now."

"And you said you'd never met your grandmother?"

"Never. Mom talked about her sometimes, but we never went to see her. I just assumed she lived really far away."

"Did your mother get letters from her?"

Jette shook her head. "I suppose something happened between them. Maybe Grandma didn't like my father, either. Maybe she kicked my mother out when she started dating him. I have no idea." Suddenly she snapped her fingers. "But that reminds me! I had something to tell you."

Great, Nate thought. Something to do with Jeanette, no doubt. "What's that?"

"I drove out to Grandma's place again, just to putter around, and there was some weird guy hanging around."

Nate wondered how Jette would define *weird.* "What was he doing?"

"I don't really know." She wrinkled her forehead. "He was kind of hanging around the edge of the yard. He stood there watching me like I was the weirdo."

Nate suppressed a laugh. "Okay, I'll look into it."

Jeanette didn't meet him so enthusiastically. She was polite this time, but Nate thought she put on a courteous facade to avoid trouble because she was already on his bad side. Jeff Lewis brought them coffee in the lodge's cozy library and left them to talk in private.

"Tell me about your childhood, Jeanette." Nate settled back in his chair with his mug cradled in both hands. He'd proposed to Emily here at the lodge, but he determined not to let thoughts like that distract him now.

"I grew up with my parents," she said. "I'm the oldest of four."

"Brothers or sisters?" Nate asked. "Or both?"

"Two brothers and a sister. But I really don't see what this has to do with anything. Have you people gotten anywhere with proving that Jette person is an impostor?"

Nate struggled not to squirm. "I'm just trying to shed some light on the situation. What can you tell me about your grandmother?"

"Nothing, really." Jeanette frowned down at her steaming mug. "I never met her. As far as I know, she never even called us or sent birthday cards."

"Mr. Wolfe told me that you claim Stella Lessard was your mother's mother. If your mom never told you about Stella, how did you even know you had a grandmother up here?"

"That's kind of a long story."

"I have time," said Nate.

Jeanette sighed. "Last year I applied to join the army. I wanted to get away from home after I graduated from high school, but I didn't think my grades were good enough for college. Of course, when I went to the recruiting center, I had to present my birth certificate. Well, that's when things started getting sticky. Dad didn't want to give me a copy of the birth certificate at first. I kept after him, and finally he gave it to me. I got a shock. Apparently my mom is really my stepmother, and I had no clue about it all those years. No one ever told me."

Nate nodded. John Wolfe had told him the bare-bones version of her story that morning. "Did you ask your parents about this?"

"I tried talking to Dad," Jeanette said. "But he refused to volunteer anything about my birthmother. He only said their marriage didn't last long, and he got custody of me. But I've been doing some research on my own since then."

"What did you find out?"

She looked away. "Not a whole lot. I still have a lot of questions."

"There's one thing that puzzles me about your story," Nate said.

"Only one?"

He smiled. "Well, one that bothers me more than the rest. Your birthmother's name on the certificate — it wasn't Lois."

Jeanette's face drooped. "No. Her name was Julia Bradley. Someone I've never heard of. But when we heard on the news the other day about Stella Lessard dying, my father insisted that she was my grandmother, and that my birthmother was Stella Lessard's daughter."

They sat in silence for a moment as Nate thought that over. Could Stella have had two daughters? "You didn't end up in the military, did you?"

Jeanette ducked her head. "No, they wouldn't take me. When I had the physical, they found out I had a heart murmur, and they didn't like that, so I got the boot. I was very disappointed after all I'd gone through to get my dad's permission to enlist."

"I'm sorry to hear that," said Nate. He would have been pretty upset if a medical condition had thwarted his dreams of becoming a police officer. Jeanette must feel like she'd failed at everything she'd tried. Except one, maybe. "But you got a job at the daycare center."

Her features lit. "Yeah. I love my job."

"That's good. It's great when you find something you really like." He eyed her pensively. The two girls' stories still had him baffled.

Nate drove out to Stella's house around four o'clock. As he pulled into the driveway, he sighted the subject of Jette's concern: Cedar Sproul.

Cedar dodged toward the woods when he saw Nate.

"Wait up!" Nate hollered after him. He

really didn't feel like chasing him down. "Hey, Cedar, don't give me trouble. Come on!"

Cedar slowed to a stop and let Nate catch up to him near the back of the house.

"Jette Williams told me you were hanging around bothering her when she was over here. What's going on?"

Cedar glared at him. "Who is she?"

"She says she's Stella's granddaughter." Nate watched him carefully.

"She shouldn't be here." Cedar turned to look at the cottage. "I'm going to get this house. The lawyer told me so."

"Mr. Wolfe said you would inherit the house if Stella's heir didn't show up within a year," said Nate. "At this point, the house is not any more yours than it is Jette's. And Cedar, you know you aren't supposed to tell anyone that you're mentioned in Stella's will."

Cedar didn't answer. He stared at the ground, rubbing the toe of his holey sneaker in the weeds.

"I want you to stay away from here and leave that girl alone," said Nate. "There might be other people, too. The lawyer will tend to things. You just stay away, understand?"

After a moment, Cedar nodded.

"All right. Now, get a move on. If I catch you hanging around here again, I'll have to arrest you." A twinge of sadness washed over Nate as he watched Cedar fade into the woods. He got into the cruiser and drove to the newspaper office. Emily practically dived at him with a barrage of questions.

"What happened with the girls? Did you find out anything? What did they say?"

He smiled halfheartedly. He wished he still had her energy at the end of the day. "This whole thing has got me really confused." He sank into a chair. "Both of them seem to have legitimate stories, however strange."

"Felicia and I think you should do DNA testing," said Emily.

"Oh, really?" Nate eyed Felicia, who was sitting at her desk pretending to mind her own business. "Are you two thinking of starting up your own detective agency?"

"Now, Nate," Emily said, "for all we know, both girls could be lying. They could have gotten false documents somehow. Or they could both be named Jeanette Williams and neither one of them might be related to Stella. Maybe they saw an opportunity to get something for nothing."

"One or both of them is being really sneaky," said Felicia.

"I agree," said Emily. "And I think there's

a lot more investigating to do."

"Now, wait a second," said Nate, beginning to feel cornered. "I just got through talking to *both* of them again. Doesn't that count for something?"

"DNA, DNA," Felicia chanted. She wiggled her eyebrows up and down.

Nate shook his head, fighting the urge to laugh. "I swung by Stella's again before coming here. Jette told me she saw someone hanging around, and when I got to the house, Cedar was there."

"She was probably trying to distract you from your real job in this case," said Felicia.

"No, I think Cedar's up to something. He seems to be there every time someone else is. I think he imagines he's keeping guard over the property."

"He's harmless," said Emily. "He did give me quite a scare the day Stella died, but I'm sure he means well." She leaned forward, resting her elbows on her desk and her head in her hands. "Nate, I really do think you should ask the girls for DNA samples. It's the quickest way to find out who's lying."

Nate knew she was right. He was getting a little tired of interviewing the two Misses Williams. "I guess I can ask." Resigned to a new round of encounters, he pushed to his feet and put his hat on.

7

"What can I tell ya?" Nate asked with a shrug that evening. "Jette let me take the cheek swab with no fuss, but Jeanette refused. And we don't have a court order, so there's nothing I can do."

Emily frowned over that and took a bite of her sandwich. Nate had offered to feed her supper tonight if she fed him the next day, when they planned to help Raven Miller move supplies to the camping center on Grand Cat. They sat on the back deck of the marina house, looking out over the lake.

"There's got to be a way. On TV they say you can collect DNA if the person throws something away."

"Oh, you want me to follow Jeanette around and pick her used tissues out of the trash? I think she'd get a little suspicious."

"No, but there's got to be a way." Emily sat up straighter in her deck chair. "I know. I'll go out to the lodge and see her before I go back to the island."

"You want me to go?"

"No. She doesn't like you. Not that she likes me that much, either, but I think she'll be more open with me than with the cop who busted her on her way into town."

"Point taken. So, do you want me to give you a swab kit? You could take it along with you, but I doubt you can get her to agree to let you use it on her."

"No. I'm not going that route. Just give me an evidence bag."

"For what? Used chewing gum?"

Lisa Cookson, the lodge's desk clerk, general help, and owner's girlfriend, welcomed Emily when she entered the lobby at Lakeview Lodge.

"Well, hi, Emily. What brings you here?"

"I wanted to see Jeanette Williams."

"Let's see, she was down for dinner about an hour ago. I haven't seen her since. I can call her room and see if she's in."

"Thanks." Emily sat on one of the loveseats before the native stone fireplace, marveling that the rustic old lodge had a telephone in every guest room now.

A moment later, Lisa came over from the desk. "Miss Williams will be right down."

"Thanks. Oh, Lisa —" Emily looked up

into the girl's dark eyes. "Is it possible for Jeanette and me to get some cold drinks served in here while we talk?"

"Certainly. What would you like? Iced tea? Diet cola?"

"Either, so long as you have straws in them."

"Straws?" Lisa's eyebrows shot up.

"Yeah. If it's not too much trouble." Emily took a five-dollar bill from her purse.

"Oh, that's okay, Emily. We serve our guests snacks all the time." Lisa moved away toward the kitchen but paused at the hallway and looked back.

Emily threw her a quick smile as she put away her money. *All right, Lord, it's not like I'm going to lie to Jeanette. So why do I feel so guilty?* She exhaled and slumped against the back of the loveseat. *Okay, I get it. Deception. Show me a better way, then.*

Jeanette came slowly down the stairs, scanning the lobby. Her gaze lit on Emily and she frowned.

"Emily Gray. Did you want to see me?"

"Yes, actually I did." Emily stood and extended her hand. "I suppose we've been pestering you a lot since you got here yesterday."

"Well, Officer Holman was here again this afternoon. I've told him and the attorney everything. I don't understand why we can't just get on with it. I'd at least like to see inside my grandmother's house before I have to leave."

"How long are you planning to stay?" Emily asked.

"Originally, I thought I'd go home Sunday. But if things aren't settled by then, I may call my boss and ask if I can have next week off."

Emily nodded. "It may take a few days for Mr. Wolfe to verify your documents."

"I'm sure he's looking closely at that Jette girl's papers, too." Jeanette sighed and plopped down on the loveseat. "Why did she have to do this? It's messing up everything."

"What do you mean?"

"I only found out about my grandmother recently, and she's dead. I hoped to come here and learn about her. You know, see her house; maybe find some photos of her. I want to know what she was like. I keep thinking about her — what she would wear; what kind of food she liked; and if I look like her."

Emily smiled suddenly. "I may be able to help you with one of those questions, Jeanette. Last fall, Stella was on a committee for the Friends of the Library club. They hosted a poetry reading, and I took some photos for the paper. I'm sure we have them on file at the office, and there may be some other pictures of Stella in our morgue." She thought that might sound ghoulish to someone whose relative had just died, so she added quickly, "That's our file of old clippings and photos."

Jeanette gave her a faint smile. "I've heard that term. That would be wonderful, if you could show me some of that stuff."

"No problem. And I think Nate said there were a few pictures of Stella and her husband — Edgar Lessard, that is — in the house. Maybe he could get permission to remove them so that you and —" Emily caught her breath. "So that you could see them."

"You were going to say so that Jette and I could see them, weren't you?"

Emily looked down at her hands and gritted her teeth. "Yeah. But only because at this stage, I'm trying to keep an open mind and treat you both equally. I'm sorry, but until Mr. Wolfe announces that he's found the heir —"

Lisa entered the room with a tray. "Here we are, ladies. Iced tea with lemon. It's not sweetened, but I brought some sugar and sweetener packets in case you want it."

"Thank you so much, Lisa," Emily said.

Lisa set the tray on the coffee table with a smile and left them. Emily leaned forward and fished a couple of sweetener packets out of the dish and tore them open.

"I hope you don't mind — I thought maybe we'd like something to drink while we talked, so I asked Lisa to bring this."

"Actually, that looks pretty good." Jeanette reached for her glass and used the straw to poke the lemon wedge beneath the surface of the liquid. "I've felt like an outcast since I got here. Like everyone sees me as an outsider who doesn't belong."

"I'm sorry you feel that way. I won't say the people of Baxter are the warmest crowd I've ever met, but I'd like to think we make visitors feel welcome."

Jeanette shrugged and sipped her tea through the straw.

Emily couldn't help thinking about the DNA evidence Jeanette was leaving. Although it was tempting, she still felt she shouldn't use the underhanded method of getting the evidence for Nate. Even if it were legal, would God want her to deliberately deceive Jeanette? She took a drink and studied the young woman's face. "Have you had a chance to go out on the lake yet?"

"No, I spent the morning in the next

town. Aswontee, is it?"

Emily nodded. "I think it's some sort of Indian name — or, more likely, a corruption of one."

"I didn't sleep well last night, so I lay down in my room this afternoon, after Officer Holman left, and I fell asleep. I woke up just in time for dinner. And then I called home to let my mom and dad know I'm okay."

"It must have been a little scary, coming all the way up here by yourself."

Jeanette poked at the lemon wedge again, stuffing it down between the ice cubes with the end of her straw. "It was a challenge, but I really wanted to do it. And of course there's the possibility that Grandmother left me something. All the way up here, I kept thinking about that, but it didn't seem real. Not until I saw her house. I mean, wow! I could own a house. Imagine."

"That's right. If your papers pass muster with Mr. Wolfe, I expect you'll be named heir to the estate."

"That would be neat." Jeanette flicked a glance at her. "But not as neat as meeting Grandma would have been. I don't know why Dad never told me about her, but he didn't, so I just have to take it as it comes."

"Right."

"But that other girl . . ." Jeanette swiveled around to face Emily. "The attorney said there could be others, too. More people trying to claim the estate, I mean. It's not like Grandmother was rich, but there is the house, and the attorney says there's some cash and investments. I suppose some people might figure it was worth a shot to say they were related to her."

"Yes." Emily leaned toward her. "Jeanette, this request of Nate's for a DNA sample is something that would help you prove your claim."

"I don't know. It seems kind of 'Big Brother' to me. Why can't they just accept my birth certificate, driver's license, and Social Security card? I don't like the idea of putting my DNA out there."

"Well, it's up to you, but I assure you they're not going to use it for anything other than to establish whether or not Stella was truly your grandmother."

Jeanette pressed her lips together for a moment. "It's just so . . . I mean, what if they made a mistake? I've heard things like that. The lab could say she wasn't related to me when she really was, you know?"

"That's very rare."

"Is it? I've read there are lots of mistakes like that — mislabeling, or contaminating the samples. I just don't feel comfortable with it."

"Okay. It's totally your decision." Emily rose with a smile. "I'm glad I had a chance to talk to you again, Jeanette. And if you do have to wait a few days, I suggest you have fun while you're here. It's a little early for swimming yet — the water takes a while to warm up in this big lake. But the lodge has boats and canoes, and there are some wonderful hiking trails here. Nate and I went snowshoeing last winter and saw a moose."

"I'm not sure I want to see the wildlife real close, but I might try a rowboat or something."

"Well, if you get out to Grand Cat, I have a cottage there," Emily said. "Stop in and see me."

"Oh, you . . . live on the island?"

"Yes, in the summer. Nate and I are getting married in August, and we'll live in the house beside the marina after that. It's where he grew up."

"Are there a lot of people on the island?" Jeanette asked.

"No, only a few cottages. Most of Grand Cat is owned by the Surpassing Peace camping center."

"It must be nice." Jeanette's voice was so

wistful that Emily felt a little guilty. A lot of hardworking families in Maine couldn't afford to summer on the beautiful lakes.

"Well, I'll see you around. I hope you'll come to the Sunday services at the church. Sunday school is at ten, and the worship service is at eleven."

Jeanette's smile looked a little strained, and Emily was sure she wouldn't come.

On Saturday morning Nate and Emily took two boatloads of supplies out to Raven's beach and helped her unload the cartons. Raven also took her own craft — a bright red speedboat — back and forth from the mainland to Grand Cat.

"We can just store everything in the lodge and the guest house," Raven told them. "I've got staffers arriving tomorrow, and we'll get everything sorted out and put away, but this is a huge help to me. Having all this stuff moved out here before they arrive puts me way ahead of schedule."

"You've got enough food here for an army." Nate hefted a carton marked SPAGHETTI SAUCE, 24–32 OZ. and headed up the path toward the log building where Raven's guests would eat their meals.

"That's good. We'll need it." Raven wrestled with a carton marked DECAFFEIN-

ATED COFFEE, GROUND, 6-3 LB. "I expect my first church group to arrive Memorial Day weekend, and we want to be ready. That's only two weeks away. We need to get the cabins cleaned and prepare the tenting sites, too."

"How many people do you expect?" Emily snapped a picture of Raven hoisting the box, pocketed her camera, and grabbed a carton of cereal.

"Forty."

"Well, that's almost an army," Nate said, turning around on the path.

Raven laughed. "Yeah, isn't it great? I was afraid it would be hard to get people to come when I changed my focus here, but several churches have booked retreats and family camp times. This group's pastor is coming with them, but the next week we're having a guest speaker in. I have a church group of about twenty-five people coming, but I want to invite the whole community. You'll give me some publicity for the evangelist, won't you, Emily?"

"You bet." Emily saw another boat heading toward the island. She waved at Marvin and Truly Vigue, her summer neighbors, and followed Nate and Raven up the lodge steps and around to the kitchen door. "Looks like the Vigues are moving to the island today, too. Their boat's riding low in the water."

Nate chuckled. "Must have brought all Truly's new accessories. Either that or Rocky's sitting down in the back of the boat."

Emily shot him a reproachful glance and told Raven, "Connie had one of those decorating home parties last month, and I thought Truly was going to buy one of everything."

"I'll invite them to come to the meetings," Raven said. "I hope the Kimmels and Mr. Rowland are here by then. Oh, and if the new guy at Derbin's is still here, I'll ask him, too."

Half an hour later, they slowly toiled up the path with the last of the boxes.

"You guys are great," Raven said. "As soon as we get these put away, I'll fix lunch. Tuna salad sandwiches okay?"

"Sounds terrific," Nate said.

"I brought some cookies," Emily added.

Over lunch, Raven asked Nate how his new job was going.

"I love it. Of course, there are some days when things get kind of kooky."

"Like Thursday," Emily said.

"What happened Thursday?" Raven looked from Emily to Nate and back again.

"Well, you heard about Stella Lessard, right?" Nate asked.

"Oh, yeah, I read yesterday's *Journal*. Two potential heirs. That's exciting."

"Yes, it was very exciting for Nate," Emily said with a smile. "He stopped one of them for speeding, and then he had to keep them from killing each other when they met."

Nate swallowed a bite of his sandwich. "I'll just be glad when the lawyer decides who's the real deal and this is over."

"Can't they go by the women's birth certificates?" Raven asked.

"Well, their birth certificates appear to be identical. Both have the same parents' names — Nicholas Williams and Julia Bradley Williams. But anyone can get a copy of a birth certificate." Nate shook his head. "Our department has been looking into it some. The sheriff says no one's committed a crime yet —"

"Other than speeding," Emily put in.

"Yeah, right. But this might turn into a case of fraud. So we're cooperating with the attorney and sharing information with him."

Raven's pupils widened. "Cool. What have you found out so far, or can you tell me?"

"Well, the weirdest thing to me is that Stella named her daughter in her will — Lois Pressey — but neither of the two girls claiming to be heirs has a mother by that name."

"That is odd."

"That's why the lawyer's taking his time. He doesn't want to make a mistake."

Emily reached for the plastic bag of cookies she'd brought and opened it. "I did some research on my own yesterday. I found out that a Stella Pressey did give birth to a daughter, whom she named Lois, forty years ago, at Mercy Hospital in Portland."

"So . . . where's this daughter now?" Raven asked.

Nate shrugged. "That's the question. The girl who calls herself Jette says her mother died two years ago. The one called Jeanette says she never knew her birthmother."

"Wow. Hey, the coffee's ready." Raven stood and grabbed the carafe. "Who wants some?"

Nate held out his mug. "There's something else." He glanced at Emily. "Since Stella's dead, I don't suppose it will matter if Raven knows."

"Probably not," Emily agreed, "but keep in mind that the two alleged 'granddaughters' probably don't know. I'd hate to have them learn it through the grapevine."

"Well, don't tell me if you shouldn't."

Raven poured Nate's mug full.

"No, it's okay. I know you can keep secrets." He sipped the coffee and set the mug down. "See, I made inquiries with a lot of law enforcement agencies. It's wonderful what computers can do for the police nowadays. I found out Stella was once arrested as an accessory to a crime — an armed robbery committed by her first husband."

"Wow."

Emily threw Raven a bleak smile. "It was unexpected. I mean, Stella was such a nice person. Everyone in town liked her."

"Well, apparently she wasn't always so nice," Nate said. "She sold him out, and her husband went to jail. So did Stella, but her sentence wasn't nearly as long. All of this happened way before she moved to Baxter."

"I wonder if she moved here to hide out," Emily mused.

Raven nodded over the rim of her coffee cup. "Baxter is about as off-the-beaten-path as you can get. If someone wanted to lie low for a while and escape their past, this might be a pretty good place to do that."

"Yeah. I think I'll call Augusta on Monday and see if there's a record of a divorce. I mean, she married Edgar Lessard. She must have divorced her thug of a first husband."

"Maybe not," Raven said.

"Ooh, bigamy?" Emily shivered. "The more we dig into this story, the weirder it gets."

"Yeah," Nate said. "But getting some more information from the state isn't a bad idea. See, we found out that Stella's daughter was taken away when she was arrested. The girl was put into foster care."

"You should request information from the state's Department of Human Services on the little girl," Emily said. "They wouldn't tell me, I'm sure, but if you asked for it officially . . ."

"We might have to get a warrant," Nate said. "These new privacy laws can be a pain."

"But it would be worth it," Raven said.

"Yes." Emily stared thoughtfully into her inky coffee. "I'm going to find out what happened to Lois, one way or another."

8

Sunday morning, five minutes before the worship service would begin, Nate found Emily standing in the church doorway staring out toward the parking lot, scanning the arriving parishioners.

Nate stepped up behind her. "What are you doing?" he whispered.

"I invited Jette and Jeanette," she said. "I didn't really expect them to come, but I guess I was hoping at least one of them would show."

"They don't strike me as the church type," Nate said.

Emily's expression drooped into a frown as she looked up at him. "But what is the church type, anyway? I never thought Raven would darken the door of this church, either, but her heart was really soft, and she was ready to hear about God almost as soon as I was ready to tell her."

"You're right. God knows people's hearts

a lot better than we do." He reached for her hand. "But it's time to start. Are you coming?"

Emily took one final look toward the parking lot then closed the door and walked with him into the auditorium, where they settled into the pew beside Connie.

After the service, Nate found his stepfather at the front while Emily went off to talk to Raven.

"Good sermon. I enjoyed that."

"Thank you," said Jared. "Hey, did you happen to see the young woman who slipped in late?"

"No, I didn't notice," said Nate. "Who was it?"

"I thought it might have been one of the girls claiming to be Stella's heir. I haven't met either of them, but Emily mentioned to Connie and me that she'd invited them."

Nate scanned the auditorium. "Is she still here?"

"Nope. She sneaked out as quickly as she sneaked in. She was gone before we were done with the final hymn."

"Huh. What did she look like?"

"Spiky hair. Lots of earrings."

"That's Jette. Emily will be glad to hear she showed up. I wonder why she didn't stay to say hi."

"Probably felt uncomfortable," said Jared. "A lot of people feel out of place in church, even if they're interested. By the way, have either of them mentioned anything to you about a funeral or a service for Stella?"

"No, they haven't," said Nate. "I suppose someone should ask them if they'd mind if the church did something. But on the other hand, if neither of them really is her heir, they shouldn't be making that decision."

Jared shook his head. "They sure have got people confused around here."

"Including me," said Nate.

"Yeah. I guess we'd better put off the memorial service awhile longer."

Nate nodded. "I'd better find Em. She's inviting Raven to have a barbecue with us tomorrow night."

Emily stood on a stepstool holding a paint roller soaked in cream-colored paint. She squinted at the top of the kitchen wall then slowly climbed down the stepladder and laid the roller in the tray next to the stool.

"Hmm." She tilted her head to one side and studied her work. She'd taken Monday afternoon off to work on the cottage, and she was quickly finding out that the paint job she'd planned was going to take longer than expected. Maybe Nate would offer to help her after they had supper with Raven.

Her stomach growled and she looked at her watch. It was nearly five o'clock, and Raven would arrive any minute with salad. Time to put the painting aside. She popped the roller head off the handle into the trash, took her paint tray to the sink, and rinsed it thoroughly, watching the milky stream flow down the drain.

When the tray was clean, she lit the grill outside and then returned to the kitchen. A knock sounded at the cottage door as she opened the refrigerator. "It's open!" She pulled out a pound of hot dogs and a large package of lean hamburger.

"Hi, Emily." Raven stepped inside and set her covered plastic bowl on the table. She wore a pair of khaki capri pants and a dark green T-shirt with her retreat center's logo. She flipped her long, dark hair back over her shoulder. "Wow. This looks great."

Emily offered a weak smile as she set the meat on the table. "I don't know. I'm no interior designer."

"You're doing a wonderful job," Raven assured her. "I'd hardly recognize the place. What's the color called?"

"Buttermilk. It has just a tinge of yellow in it."

"It's very light and encouraging."

"Think so?" Emily eyed the wall beside the stove again. Raven had an artistic bent, so her judgment on colors should be trustworthy.

"Yes. I think you'll enjoy working in here with it so sunny and bright." Raven grinned at her. "Hey, I thought you'd be in a frenzy writing tomorrow's front-page story."

"I finished it this morning." Emily eyed her uneasily. "Unless something unexpected happens, tomorrow's *Journal* is all set. But you know, unexpected things have been happening a lot around here lately."

Raven gave her a quick hug. "Relax and enjoy the evening. What can I do to help you?"

"Well, I've got the grill going. I hope I didn't turn the burners too high this time. If you want to get the paper plates and whatnot from the cupboard over there, I'll start cooking. Nate should be here soon."

"Okeydokey, head chef."

"Maybe you should be the guest head chef. You're better at grilling than I am. Of course, it doesn't take much to claim that honor."

Raven grinned and took down a package of plates. "I'm sure between the two of us, we can manage to cook a few burgers. Let's go."

■ ■ ■ ■

When Nate climbed out of his boat at Emily's dock, he could see that the girls were nearly done with their preparations. They had set up Emily's card table and three lawn chairs beneath the big pines by the path to the cottage. The smell of grilling beef enticed him to come closer. He stooped to pick up the cooler of soft drinks he'd brought.

"Are you lovely ladies having a picnic?" he called as he approached. "Mind if I join you?"

"As if you couldn't smell it from halfway across the lake," said Emily. "I hope you brought your appetite. I think we made too much food, and Raven made sure I didn't burn it."

"I'm always happy to solve the problem of too much food." Nate grinned. Emily looked happy, and he thought the warmer weather had done a lot to improve her spirits. That and finding what she assured him was the perfect wedding dress. She was always happiest when she could get out of the house or the office and be outside in the sunshine.

"Anything I can do, or are we ready to eat?"

Emily moved the meat from the grill to a couple of plates and set them on the table. "Uh, ketchup, mustard, relish. I think we've got everything. Who wants to pray?"

"I will," said Raven.

Emily smiled.

Nate knew she was proud of how much Raven had grown spiritually in the last year. She was so eager to talk to God, and not at all ashamed of her new faith. They bowed their heads where they stood, and Raven said the blessing. The sound of an outboard motor grew louder as she spoke.

Nate sneaked a look toward the water as Raven wound down to the amen. He was certain the approaching boat had something to do with police business. Something always seemed to come up right when he was ready to relax.

"Who's that?" Emily asked, shading her eyes against the sun with her hand. "Is it Gary?"

"Sure enough," said Nate. "And that looks like Detective Blakeney with him. This had better be important. I had my taste buds all set for a big, juicy burger."

"Why don't you ask them to join us?" Emily suggested.

"I think I will."

"I guess we don't have too much food,

after all," said Raven.

"You never did," said Nate. "I'm starving. But I'll let them each have some."

Emily laughed as the two men climbed out of the boat and started up the path from the dock.

"Hey, Gary!" Nate called. "Howdy, Detective Blakeney."

Nate's cousin, Gary Taylor, smiled and raised his hand in a casual salute. "Hello, all. Having a barbecue, I see. Nice day for it."

"You're welcome to join us," said Raven.

"Well, hi, Raven," Gary said. "We came out here to deliver something, but we might be able to have a bite with you after we talk to Nate."

Emily elbowed Nate in the ribs. He looked at her sharply. She was smiling and looking at Raven. He was sure she was trying to communicate something to him in some secret Emily language, but he had no idea what. All he saw was Raven looking a little embarrassed, or maybe she'd been standing too near the grill and the heat made her cheeks pink up like that. "What?" he whispered.

Emily shook her head as if to say, "Tell you later."

Blakeney gave the young women a curt

smile. He held a manila envelope under one arm. "Ladies. Sorry to intrude at mealtime." He drew Nate a few steps aside. "I'm sorry to bother you on your day off, too, but something big has turned up. I thought you'd want to know right away."

"Oh?" Something to do with Jette and Jeanette Williams? Nate hoped not. That could ruin his appetite.

"The toxicology report came back from the autopsy." Blakeney held out the large envelope. "It turned up something pretty interesting."

"What's that?" Nate asked, reaching for the report.

Blakeney's face showed no expression. "Stella Lessard was poisoned."

9

Emily hurried up to the cottage for more plates and silverware. When she came back down near the grill, Raven and Gary were standing on the dock together. She heard Raven's silvery laugh and smiled to herself. Maybe she wouldn't have to work too hard at this — just let nature take its course.

Nate was still huddled with Blakeney, and that duo worried her more. As she set the paper plates on the card table, she heard Blakeney say, "I'll be taking over the case for the state police. I already spoke to the sheriff about it, but I wanted to touch base with you personally. He told me I could probably find you out here."

Emily didn't look at them but ambled toward the dock. Her chest ached, and that was on Nate's behalf. Was the sheriff taking Nate off the case because of his inexperience? More likely they'd learned that Stella's death was not accidental. That would explain this visit all right. Emily hoped it wasn't true, but she couldn't think of another reason for Blakeney to take over that wouldn't mean trouble for Nate. She remembered how much Nate and Ward Delaney hated losing the Lakeview Lodge case to the state police last spring. Local officers and county sheriff's deputies weren't allowed to investigate murders. Only big city police departments and the state police had homicide detectives.

She slowed her steps, not wanting to break in on the ambiance between Raven and Gary. Even from a dozen yards away, she could see the gleam in Raven's dark eyes. The air around those two crackled with electricity. If she could harness it, she could probably light all the cottages on the island with it. At least something was going right.

Emily gulped a deep breath and looked out over her tiny beach. The water was calm, with gentle ripples of waves lapping the shore. *Make me as calm as that water, Lord,* she prayed silently. *Blakeney's got my stomach all in knots again. Why did he have to come do this, anyway? Nate was doing fine with the investigation.*

She glanced over her shoulder. Nate nodded and frowned grimly, and Blakeney talked on without a break. She could almost make out his words, but she was glad she couldn't. Not if he was chewing Nate out. It almost looked that way. Maybe he thought Nate hadn't handled things well the day they discovered Stella's body. It made her want to slap the detective. *Yeah, right. That would be really smart.*

She turned back to watch the lake. *Lord, I know Nate has You on his side. He doesn't need me to defend him.* Even so, she hoped Blakeney wouldn't bully him. Nate was still new at the job and determined to succeed. He valued the opinions of other officers. Her past experiences with Blakeney told her that he wasn't always very polite about claiming his territorial rights.

"Hey, Emily," Raven called.

Emily managed a smile and sauntered toward the dock. "What's up?"

"Gary says he'll stay and eat with us if one of us can take him home later."

"Sure. Nate will be going back to the mainland, anyway. He'll take you."

Gary grinned. "Fantastic. I was off duty officially an hour ago, but Detective Blakeney wasn't ready to quit."

"What's going on?" Raven asked.

Emily was grateful to her for voicing the question. She'd determined to leave it alone until someone else brought it up.

"That woman you found dead last week . . ." Gary looked at Emily, and she nodded. "Murdered."

"Wow," said Raven. "Really?"

"Yeah. Blakeney's the officer in charge now." He smiled at Emily and gave her shoulder a little squeeze. "Don't worry. Your honey and his department will work with us." Gary glanced up and straightened.

Emily turned toward the shore. Blakeney strode onto the dock and walked toward them, still sober-faced.

"You staying, Taylor?"

"Yes, sir. My cousin will take me home."

"All right. Good night, Miss Gray. Miss Miller." Blakeney nodded solemnly at Emily and Raven.

"Won't you have something to eat with us, Detective?" Emily asked.

"No, thank you. I'll be getting home." Blakeney climbed down into the boat he and Gary had come in — one of the Baxter Marina's rentals — and started the outboard.

Emily sighed deeply. As the boat pulled away, they all turned toward the grill and table. Nate stood waiting for them at the end of the dock.

"Think my burger's cold?" he asked.

"Probably iced over," Raven said with a laugh.

She and Gary walked on. Emily instinctively reached for Nate. He slipped his arm around her and pulled her in close to his side.

"Don't fret, Em. It's going to be okay." He kissed her hair just above her ear.

"You sure?"

"Yeah."

"Thanks." She hugged him then eased away.

"We'll talk later," he promised.

As the sun lowered behind the hill on the island, the four of them laughed and talked about everything but Stella Lessard. They stuffed themselves with burgers, hot dogs, tossed salad, and chips, after which Nate produced the makings for s'mores from his cabin cruiser.

Emily groaned. "I have ice cream in the freezer."

"Save it," Gary said. "I haven't had a s'more in ages."

"How long ago?" Raven asked. "Since you were a kid?"

"Oh, at least . . . nine months ago."

Nate laughed. "Yeah, that's about right for last year's final campfire. Gary's still just a kid. Got any marshmallow sticks, Emily?"

"No, you'll have to cut some."

"Okay, will do. Gary, do you want to get the marshmallow sticks or start the fire?"

"I guess if you're determined, we can have a fire out here." Emily nodded toward the fire pit Nate had built the summer before. "There's plenty of dry wood in the shed."

Nate nodded. "We'll get the sticks and bring a load of firewood when we come back." He and Gary took out their pocketknives and headed for the small patch of woods behind the cottage.

"Gary's a nice guy," Raven said, not quite looking at Emily.

"Yeah." Emily opened the box of graham crackers Nate had brought. Raven and Gary had met the summer before, but Emily didn't suppose their paths crossed often. Maybe they needed a little help in the path-crossing department. After all, Raven's camp was situated on an island with seven other cottages. "I was thinking of inviting him to go with Nate and me to the meetings at your retreat Memorial Day weekend."

"That would be cool." Raven sat in silence for a moment. "He *is* a Christian, right?"

"Yes, no need to worry on that account."

The sparks definitely flew while they made the s'mores, and not just from the fire pit.

When Emily extended her invitation to the camp meetings, Gary threw her a lopsided grin, but his gaze swiveled back to Raven.

"Sounds good. I'll see if I can make it."

Raven practically glowed. "Terrific. If you all can come in time for dinner, you can join the folks at the retreat for the meal."

Later, when Emily gathered an armful of dirty dishes, Nate jumped up. "I'll help you, Em."

"Me, too," said Raven.

"That's okay," Nate said. "You guys stay here. We'll be back in a sec."

Emily trudged up the path, and Nate followed her with the leftover buns, chips, and barbecuing tools.

"You shut the grill off, right?" she asked as she deposited her load of dishes on the counter.

"Yup. Long time ago." Nate set down the food and slid the tongs and spatula into the sink. "Come here, babe."

Emily glided into his arms and rested her head against his shoulder. "I'm glad Gary stayed."

"Me, too, but it means I don't get much time alone with you."

She chuckled and lifted her face to meet his kiss.

"That's better." He folded her in his arms

with a sigh.

"Is everything really okay with Blakeney?" she asked.

"Yes. It's routine when they find out it was homicide, you know?"

"Yeah, I figured that was it. What happened to her?"

"Poison."

Emily drew away from him and studied his face. "Someone . . . poisoned Stella?"

"So the medical examiner says."

"Wow."

"Yeah."

"Any idea who?"

Nate shook his head. "Of course Blakeney will interview Cedar."

"And me?"

"Probably. But he knows you didn't do it."

"Well, I doubt Cedar did. Stella was his best friend."

"I don't know about that."

"Oh, you know what I mean." She wriggled away from him and gathered plastic cups to throw in the trash. "She hired him to do handyman jobs. That may be his only income."

"No, he gets Social Security."

"Why?"

"Disabled somehow. Anyway, I don't think

we can rule him out. Cedar's mind works in a very convoluted way. Who knows what he thinks?"

She nodded, mulling that over. "But Blakeney wasn't upset with you?"

"No. Of course he wished we'd known it was a homicide from the start."

"The medical examiner who came to the scene called it an unattended death and reported no signs of foul play," she reminded him. "Even the county sheriff told you he doubted there was foul play."

"I know. Blakeney said we did all right, under the circumstances, but there were a few things he'd have done differently. And he's curious about Jette and Jeanette."

"So am I," Emily said. "I think Jette was the poisoner. Or Jeanette. I can't make up my mind which. Guess I need more evidence. I wonder if either of them had access to poison."

"Well, they've both got motive," Nate said.

"Motive." Emily sighed. "Who benefits? That's what you cops always look at first."

"With good reason. And that's certainly the big question in this case. Who would benefit — or thinks he would benefit — from Stella's death? At least Jette and Jeanette have both stayed in town voluntarily, so it won't be hard for him to interview them." Nate put his hand on his stomach. "Man, I shouldn't have eaten those last three s'mores."

She laughed and slugged his shoulder. "You'd better go collect Gary and the cooler and head for home, fella. We both have to work tomorrow. And sometime we've got to nail down the guest list for the wedding and get those invitations ready to mail."

"Oh, yeah, my mom said to tell you she's got the addresses ready and she'll bring them to you at the *Journal* office tomorrow." He stood looking at her for a moment with the soft smile that almost melted her. "Hey, did you notice? Gary and Raven sort of . . . you know. Click."

Emily stood on tiptoe to kiss him. "Yeah, I noticed. Come on."

10

Nate's shoulders slumped as he left John Wolfe's office in Aswontee late Tuesday morning. The pavement in the parking area held puddles from an early morning rain. Nothing new yet on identifying the true heir, but Wolfe had advised him that the police and sheriff's department should keep a closer watch on the Lessard property. The law enforcement agencies might be open to a lawsuit from the true heir if someone else had access to it. Nate frowned as he thought of Cedar Sproul. Had he followed instructions and stayed away from Stella's house?

A dose of Emily would help right about now, but she was probably busy. He pulled out his cell phone anyhow.

Emily's cheery greeting shored him up.

"Any possibility we can have lunch together?" he asked.

"Uh, maybe, if it's a late lunch. One o'clock?"

"Sure. You want to go out?"

"Let's save money and make sandwiches," she said.

"Okay. I've got peanut butter and bologna."

"I'll stop by the store for some ham salad if it's all the same to you."

"Whatever you want. Look, I've got to go out to the lodge and see Jeanette again. Pray that she'll speak to me, okay?"

"I thought you'd be over at Stella's house, helping Blakeney."

"They have the mobile crime lab out there, but we county boys are stuck with interviewing neighbors and claimants to the estate. There's a new one, by the way."

"Another grandchild?"

"No," Nate said. "It's Edgar Lessard's brother. Seems his attorney contacted John Wolfe saying they think the will is unenforceable and should be declared null and void. Wilbur Lessard is putting in a claim in case Stella's daughter is never found."

"But . . . he's not even related to her."

Nate grimaced. "He's claiming it as Edgar's estate. When Edgar died, he didn't know about Stella's daughter. He left his full estate to Stella, or to his brother if Stella predeceased him."

"Oh." Emily was quiet for a moment. "So

128

Wilbur figures he's next in line, even though Stella left a will to the contrary?"

"Wolfe says the judge will throw out his claim, because Edgar's estate already passed to Stella. But it's more red tape and more time in court."

"Won't the lawyer's fees drain Stella's estate?"

Nate inhaled and looked around to make sure no one was standing near him in the parking area. "No, Wolfe tells me it won't. Seems it's more . . . extensive than we thought."

The gravel parking lot at Lakeview Lodge was dark from the early rain. Nate got out of his county car and went inside. Behind the desk, Lisa Cookson was checking in a couple of guests. She glanced at Nate, smiled, and waved him toward Jeff's office.

"Well, hi, Nate." Jeff rose from behind his cluttered desk and shook his hand. "What brings you out here?"

"I'd like to see Miss Williams if she's in."

"Why am I not surprised?"

Nate sat in the chair opposite the desk, and Jeff resumed his seat. "She hasn't been any trouble, has she?"

"Not a bit. She was out for a while yesterday, but this morning one of our staff actually talked her into a canoeing lesson."

"Wow, that's great."

"Uh-huh. They're out on the lake now. You know Ginny Walsh?"

"Yeah," Nate said.

"She's on our housekeeping staff, but she's a good canoeist, too. I'm glad she's got Miss Williams interested in some outdoor recreation. Maybe she'll see this as a vacation, not just a business trip. Could lead to more business for us later, from her friends and family. Word of mouth, that's the best advertising."

"Sounds good to me."

Jeff glanced at his watch. "They've been out for more than half an hour. They'll probably take a break soon. And Ginny will help serve lunch today."

"I'll go down to the beach and see if they've come in yet." Nate left his friend and ambled outside and down to the dock. It was a nice aluminum dock system with a Fiberglas deck, one Jeff had ordered through the Baxter Marina two years ago. Nate had helped install it. It still looked terrific. He tested it by bouncing up and down. It felt solid.

He didn't really want to talk to Jeanette again, but Blakeney had asked him to touch base with her and Jette while he got an overview of the crime scene, read all of Nate and Ward's previous reports, and did his initial investigation at the Lessard property. Nate's instructions were to tell the girls that Stella's death had been ruled a homicide — no details — and inform them that they needed to stay in Baxter for a few more days. Blakeney would catch up to them later today, or Wednesday at the latest, for a complete interview.

Nate walked out to the wide part of the wharf, where they docked small motorboats and canoes. In the distance he could see a couple of boats near the swampy area at the southwest end of the lake. Fishermen. He shaded his eyes and looked out toward Grand Cat. Sure enough, a canoe with two life-jacketed occupants was approaching from around the far side of the island. He watched them for a few minutes. Ginny sat in the stern. That was obvious from the strength and confidence with which she paddled. The girl in the front stroked less vigorously. Jeanette must be getting tired.

He heard their laughter across the water, and he was glad. They were close enough now that he could see Jeanette's face. She looked more relaxed than he'd ever seen her before — almost happy.

Until she glanced toward the dock and

saw him.

Jeanette's smile faded, and she froze with her paddle in midair. Nate left the dock and walked onto the sandy strip where they would land.

"Just lay your paddle across the thwarts," Ginny called to Jeanette. "I'll bring us in." The canoe glided up to shore and the bow scraped the sand. Nate grabbed the front and pulled it up onto the beach.

"Hi, Miss Williams. Looks like you're enjoying the lake this morning."

"Yes, I was, Officer," Jeanette said.

He offered her his hand as she prepared to climb out onto the beach. She looked at his outstretched arm for a second and slowly reached to accept his help.

"Is there news about my grandmother?" she asked.

"Yes. I'd like to talk to you for just a few minutes."

Ginny walked forward in the canoe, holding the gunwales, climbed out, and grinned at him. "Hi, Nate. Jeanette, I can take your life jacket up to the lodge for you. I need to get into the kitchen."

"Sure." Jeanette unbuckled her orange life jacket and handed it to Ginny. "Thanks. And thanks for the lesson."

"It was fun," Ginny said. "If you're not

too sore tomorrow, we'll go out again, okay? I can show you where the herons have their nests."

"I'd like that."

Ginny went up the path swinging the extra life jacket. Nate waited until Jeanette turned to face him.

"What is it, Officer Holman?"

"Would you like to go sit on the porch?" He didn't think Jeanette would faint when he told her the news, but his training told him to get her away from the water and preferably sitting down. They walked up the path together in silence.

When they were seated in the comfortable rocking chairs on the lodge's porch, Nate smiled ruefully at her. "This isn't good news, and I'm sorry to have to give it to you. The medical examiner released his autopsy report to the police yesterday. Based on his findings, Mrs. Lessard's death has been reclassified as a homicide."

Jeanette inhaled sharply. "She was murdered?"

"Yes."

"How?"

"The detective in charge will tell you everything when he comes to interview you. His name is Orson Blakeney, and he's with the Maine state police. He's very thorough, very competent. I've worked with him on other cases before, and I can assure you he'll do everything possible to find who's responsible for Mrs. Lessard's death."

She nodded. "Do they have any suspects?"

"I can't tell you that. But the news that it was a homicide will get out, and I'm sure Detective Blakeney will hold some press conferences about the investigation. He'll tell you everything he can when he comes to see you."

"I'm her granddaughter."

Nate hesitated, looking into her eyes. She didn't look away. Softly, he said, "I'm sorry, but you know we can't accept that until your documents are verified. And even if your birth certificate is genuine, there's still no proof you're the victim's granddaughter."

She dropped her gaze then. "Lois. That was her daughter's name."

"Yes."

Jeanette sighed. "I told you about my shock when I learned that my mother — the only mother I ever knew — wasn't really my mother at all." She bit her bottom lip. "Still, I thought when I came here . . ." She looked up at him earnestly. "The name on my birth certificate is different. It says my mother's name was Julia Bradley. Not Lois Lessard, or whatever her last name was."

Nate nodded. "See, that's a problem. But the attorney and the police are working on it. We all hope to see this cleared up soon."

"And what about . . . you know. That other girl. The one who calls herself Jette Williams. What does *her* birth certificate say?"

Nate gritted his teeth. "I'm sorry. I can't discuss that with you."

"Well, I figure it doesn't have the right name, either, or they'd have named her Grandmother's heir by now. I'm telling you, she's lying."

Nate's adrenaline started to flow. Time to escape. He got to his feet. "Thanks for your time, Miss Williams. The detective will come around later today or tomorrow to see you, and you can ask him your questions. If you're really Stella's granddaughter, then time is on your side. Let the police work this out."

Emily and Nate ate their sandwiches on the back deck of the marina house. The clouds had fled, and the sun warmed Emily's bare arms. She kicked off her shoes with a sigh.

"Summer. I love it."

Nate chuckled. "It won't officially be summer for another month."

"I know. But this is the start of it. May is

my favorite month. No more ice and snow for five or six months, and the blackflies aren't out yet."

"So, what are you doing this afternoon?" Nate asked before he took another bite of his ham salad sandwich.

"I'm supposed to take some pictures at the elementary school and write up a story on the students of the month. Then I'm taking the rest of the afternoon off until Blakeney's press conference."

"I don't suppose you'd want to run over to the Heron's Nest with me?"

"The Heron's Nest? Oh." She tried to scowl at him but couldn't keep from smiling. "You're afraid of Jette, aren't you?"

"No. Well, not really." Nate shrugged. "She's a little overpowering."

"Blakeney's making you talk to her again?"

"Yeah, it's my job to tell them we're looking at murder now. I saw Jeanette this morning."

"How did that go?"

"Not too badly. She was actually . . ."

"Civil?"

"Yeah. I almost said 'nice.' But Jette comes on so strongly. Like she's my best buddy because she got here first."

Emily studied his face. "But now you

think Jeanette is the one who's telling the truth?"

"I don't know what to think. I'm inclined toward saying they're both impostors. But Jeanette . . . I think she believes it. At least she wants to. Her jerk of a father pulled the rug out from under her, and now she wants roots."

"Yeah." Emily didn't like to think about stepfamilies and broken homes. She still felt guilty over the relief she'd felt when her own stepfather died. If Jeanette's story was true, she'd never had the opportunity to know her real mother. "Well, think about this, honey. If Stella was poisoned —"

"Sh!" Nate looked over toward the marina dock, but no one was within earshot. "We're not supposed to leak it until Blakeney makes the announcement tonight."

"Sorry. We can't break it in print until Friday, anyway. The daily papers have a real advantage over us this time. But as I was saying, if the method was the one you told me about earlier, how could either one of those girls possibly have done it?"

Nate popped the last bite of his sandwich into his mouth and stared out over the lake as he chewed and swallowed. "I have no clue. Maybe it was slow-acting and they came around last week and did it, then left again. Or maybe the one who did it met Stella someplace else and is just pretending never to have met her before."

"Does Blakeney know how the poison was administered?"

"If he does, he hasn't passed that on. But we do know the autopsy report said she had a high dose of Procaine in her system."

"What's that?"

"Some cocaine derivative."

"Cocaine? In Baxter?"

That had troubled Nate, too. "It's not a street drug. It would have to be obtained from a pharmacy or hospital, and it could cause anaphylactic shock pretty quickly. I don't know what to think. But that's why Blakeney's on the case now, not me."

"Do I detect a hint of envy in that remark?"

"No. It's just . . . he has the training. He knows how to solve a case like this."

"Being a sheriff's deputy isn't going to be enough for you, is it?"

"I love being a deputy."

Emily reached over and squeezed his hand. "You should be a detective."

"That won't happen in Baxter."

"I know." She sat back and closed her eyes, feeling the warm sun and listening to the waves sloshing against the dock pilings.

"So maybe we won't stay here forever. Maybe after a few years, you'll need to go to Bangor or Portland or the state police."

"I'm not even thinking about it, Em." Nate helped himself to a cookie from the plastic container his mother had dropped off the day before.

"Not yet," Emily said. "It's okay."

"You gave up Hartford and came back to Hicksville for me. I'm not going to ask you to leave Baxter again."

She let that cycle in her mind, eyes still closed against the brilliant sun on water. She loved Baxter. This was home. She didn't want to leave again. With Nate's hand in hers, she envisioned their future. If he pursued a career as a detective, she could go back to the excitement of working for a big daily newspaper. But did she want that? What about the babies they both hoped for? She'd dreamed of raising her children on the island.

"It's okay," she said again. "We'll keep the cottage."

11

Emily steered her boat toward Raven's beach. She'd left work early to go with Nate when he broke the news of the murder to Jette, but Jette wasn't at the Heron's Nest. Rita Eliot had no idea where she'd gone, so Nate had left to patrol, and Emily had wearily climbed into her boat. The sun glared on the water and baked her skin. She should have packed sunscreen. Halfway to the island she'd decided to visit Raven and see how many of the staff had arrived, and what progress they'd made in preparations for the first group of campers.

"Oh, hi, Emily," Raven called when she peered in through the back screen door of the camp kitchen. "Come on in. This is our cook for the season, Brant Lucas."

"Hello, Mr. Lucas," Emily said to the gray-haired man.

"Hi, there." His decidedly Maine accent turned "there" into "they-uh," and Emily grinned. She was glad Raven wasn't bringing in a fancy chef this year, as she had when she'd run New Age–themed retreats for women only.

"How's it going?"

"Great," Raven replied. "Brant's wife is in the office preparing brochure mailings for me. I've got two girls cleaning the guest cottages and a young man sprucing up the tenting area. I thought I might hire one of the Thibault boys to help put the dock in and mow around the lodge. Do you think they're old enough?"

"Probably. Why don't you ask their parents next time you're on the mainland? They'd probably love to come out here for a day."

Raven nodded. "If they work hard, I'll let them swim afterward. The water's getting warm enough."

"Jonathan Woods would probably come help with the dock," Emily said. "Nate, too, if it's in the morning, before his shift starts."

Raven's eyes widened. "Hey, that reminds me. I saw a girl driving a boat along the shore of the island right after lunch. She had a bunch of earrings and face rings, and I thought maybe she was that punk girl Nate was talking about the other night. Short hair, black sweatshirt."

"It sounds like Jette Williams." Emily

frowned. "Nate was looking for her a little while ago. Did you see where she went?"

"No, I didn't see her put in, but she was headed that way." Raven pointed toward the south end of the island. "Maybe she was just out for the fun of it, or . . ."

"Do you think she might have gone over to Lakeview Lodge on the south shore?" Emily asked.

"Well . . . I thought at the time that she was going to Henry Derbin's cottage. She was going really slow and watching the shore as if she was looking for something. I didn't see her swing around and head back toward Baxter. But I came inside a few minutes later. I suppose she might have gone over to Lakeview Lodge."

Emily weighed the new information in her mind.

"Hey," Raven asked, "do you want to go get your swimsuit and come back for a dip?"

Emily shivered. "Too chilly for me yet, though it sounds like fun. I think I'd better go back to the mainland and call Nate. He was supposed to talk to Jette Williams about Stella today." Not for the first time, she wished they could get phone service on Grand Cat. Of course, she and Nate would talk a blue streak then. "Thanks, Raven." She hurried down to the beach and pushed off her boat. The motor started on the first try, for which she was thankful. She turned her head so that her hair blew out behind her. How much damage were the wind and sun doing to her hair? She added conditioner to her mental shopping list, along with an extra bottle of sunscreen to keep in the boat. The ride across the mile of water to the marina was uneventful, and as soon as she cut the engine and tied up, she dashed down the street to Blue Heron Realty.

Bridget Kaplin looked up as she entered. "Well, hello, Emily. What brings you here? I gave Charlie my ad copy this morning."

"I'm not here about that, but thanks for advertising with the *Journal*. Actually I was wondering about a client of yours. Specifically, the gentleman renting Henry Derbin's cottage on Grand Cat."

"You mean Paulie Derbin's cottage," Bridget said with a sad smile.

"Yes, of course."

"It takes getting used to, doesn't it? Henry being gone, I mean."

"His death affected a lot of Baxter people," Emily said.

"True. However, I can't tell you who's renting the cottage now. Professional ethics. We have to respect the client's confidentiality. And this client specified he wanted a secluded spot where he could rest."

"I see." Emily ran a hand through her shoulder-length hair, considering that. Bridget didn't seem willing to budge. "Well, thank you."

She went outside and stood on the sidewalk for a moment then took out her cell phone and called Nate. He agreed to meet her at his house, and she went to the marina for cold drinks. Fifteen minutes later, Nate and Ward Delaney drove into the marina parking lot in the sheriff's department car. She met them at the side of the house, and they all went out to the back deck, where Emily had set out sodas and a plate of Connie's cookies.

"Seems like a wild speculation that she went to Derbin's place," Ward said when Emily relayed what Raven had told her.

"Yeah." Nate shook his head, frowning. "We have no proof it was Jette, either."

"Yes, we do." Emily smiled in triumph. "If it was her, where would she get a boat?"

"The marina," Nate said.

"Right. When I went to get the sodas, I asked Allison if Jette had come in and rented a boat today. Seems Allison isn't as picky about customer privacy as Bridget is. She told me the spike-haired girl with all the jewelry stuck in her face took out a boat around twelve thirty and brought it back just before two o'clock."

"Hmm. Twelve bucks rental," Nate mused.

Emily smiled. "Allison only charged her for one hour."

"Okay. What else?"

"She showed me the rental log. Jette Williams. And she said Jon went out to the dock and made sure she had a life jacket and knew how to handle the outboard. They didn't watch to see where she went."

"So we still don't know that she went to see the renter. We don't even know who he is."

"I called Jeff, and she did *not* go to Lakeview Lodge. Can't you get a warrant?" Emily asked, looking from him to Ward. "Make Bridget tell you his name."

"Why?" Nate asked. "The guy hasn't done anything. A judge isn't going to give us a warrant to let us bother a man just because a nosy neighbor thinks someone went to see him."

Ward cleared his throat. "Warrants aren't issued lightly. Nate is right about that. But maybe you and Nate could pay this gent a visit."

Emily eyed him for a long moment. "You mean, a neighborly call?"

"Sure. You live on the island. You want to meet your new neighbor and welcome him."

"Great idea. But Nate's in uniform."

"He could change," Ward said, looking pointedly over his shoulder at Nate's house.

"Well, I'm on duty," Nate said. "And I'm not supposed to do undercover work, am I?"

Ward shrugged. "You could take your supper break early."

"Yeah, I suppose I could." Nate met Emily's gaze. "I admit I'm curious about that guy. He doesn't seem to have left the island over the weekend."

"He's probably just a quiet nature lover enjoying a peaceful vacation," Ward said. "But you might as well find out. Put some jeans on, Nate. Meanwhile, I'll ride over and see Rocky Vigue. We haven't checked up on him for a while now."

"Okay," Nate said. "But if we get an emergency call . . ."

"I'll deal with it." Ward nodded and reached for another cookie as he rose. "Good cookies."

"Maybe we should take some to the renter," Emily said.

Half an hour later they docked at the Derbin cottage. Nate, in his cargo pants and

UMO sweatshirt, looked casual enough, Emily decided. She still wore the slacks, blouse, and sweater she'd worn to work that morning. Nate gave her a hand as she climbed out onto the dock and then passed her the plate of cookies they'd covered with plastic wrap.

As they walked up the path to the cottage, Emily couldn't help but recall the day they'd come to deliver Henry Derbin's mail and found him dead in his summer home. She shivered, and Nate shot her a concerned glance.

"You okay?"

"Yeah. You knock."

He rapped firmly on the door, and a man's voice called from off to one side, "Hello! Over here."

Emily swiveled and saw a man approaching slowly over the rocks along the southern tip of the island. He was tall, with a slight hunch in his shoulders, and his shaggy gray hair flew in the breeze. He wore a jacket over a sweatshirt and had a fishing hat pulled low over his ears, nearly touching the bridge of his glasses. When he reached the path, Emily studied his creased face and dark eyes. His gaze held curiosity but no warmth.

"Hello," Nate said.

Emily stepped forward, extending the plate with a smile. "Welcome. I'm Emily Gray, and this is my fiancé, Nate Holman. I have the last cottage, at the other end of the island."

"How may I help you?"

"We just stopped in to say hello and welcome," Nate said.

"And we brought you some cookies." Emily watched his face. He definitely liked the looks of Connie's oatmeal cookies with raisins.

"That's very nice of you." He took the plate and nodded at her with an almost-smile. "Thank you very much. I've been eating store-bought provisions all week."

"Do you plan to stay long?" Nate asked.

Emily was afraid his question was too direct, so she added quickly, "Nate and I are getting married the third Saturday in August. If you plan to be here all summer, of course you're invited. We'd like to share the occasion with all the island residents."

"Oh, I won't be here that long," he said regretfully. "I've rented the cottage for another week, and then I'll head back home. I'll miss it, though. It's so peaceful here. I hate to go back to civilization."

"Where's home?" she asked.

"I live outside Boston."

"This is a really big change for you, then," Nate said.

"Yes. I grew up in a small town, but not as small as Baxter. And living on an island . . . well, that idea's always intrigued me. I've enjoyed my stay tremendously."

"Have you done any fishing?" Nate asked.

"Yes, I did a little off the point this morning. Didn't catch anything, but who cares?"

"Say, would you mind . . ." Emily ducked her head and shrugged. "I hate to ask, but if you could just slide those cookies onto another plate, I could take that one back. You wouldn't have to track me down to return it, Mr. . . ." She looked up at him expectantly.

"Smithson. Anthony Smithson. Of course, I'd be happy to."

They stood aside, and he entered the kitchen. Emily hung back. She didn't think she wanted to go into Henry Derbin's cottage, although she'd visited Paulie Derbin there after her grandfather's death. Still, she couldn't help shuddering every time she saw the little house on the rocky end of the island.

Nate stepped closer and gave her a quick squeeze. "You're good," he whispered.

She felt her color rising. Of course Nate had seen through her ruse.

Smithson appeared in the doorway, carrying the empty plate. "Here you go, Miss Gray. Thank you very much for the cookies."

"You're welcome. I hope you enjoy them."

"Maybe we'll see you again before your vacation is over," Nate said.

"Maybe so."

Nate and Emily walked down to the dock. Emily carried the plate carefully, touching only the edge. When she turned to look back, Smithson still stood on the porch and raised his hand in farewell.

Nate jumped down into the boat and held up his arms. Emily hopped down into them.

"He seems like a nice guy," Nate said.

"I don't know." Emily frowned and tucked the plate carefully into a locker. "I thought when he told us his name, he was going to say 'Smith,' but then he realized that was too obvious, so he tacked on 'son.'"

Nate laughed. "Okay, Sherlock, so you think he gave us a false name."

"I do." She grinned at him. "But you'll find out, won't you?"

"You bet. Thanks to you, we got his fingerprints all over that plate."

Emily sat down on one of the seats, recalling her mental tug-of-war when she considered taking Jeanette's straw to Nate for a

DNA test. "Are you okay with that? I mean, it's not illegal to get them that way."

"No, it's not. Police do it all the time. He willingly handed you that plate. Besides, Ward agrees he's a suspicious character. With an open murder case, we need to check all possibilities."

Emily leaned back, content to watch Nate cast off and start the engine.

12

Nate and Ward got to Stella's house early Wednesday morning, just before the mobile crime lab arrived. A state trooper was already sitting in his car in the driveway, and Nate surmised he'd been on duty all night to watch the crime scene. Blakeney drove in behind the crime lab's van and unlocked the house for the crime scene investigators. When the others had gone inside, he looked at Nate and Ward, who waited beside the walkway.

"Anything we can do to help out today, Detective?" Ward asked.

Blakeney leaned against one of the posts supporting the porch roof. "We did a thorough search of the house yesterday. I'll be interviewing some of the neighbors and the four potential heirs today."

Nate did a quick mental count. Besides the two Williams girls, Blakeney must be counting Cedar Sproul and Edgar Lessard's brother.

"Have you determined the means of poisoning?" Ward asked.

"The lab in Augusta is working on it. The Procaine in her system was probably injected. That's the way it's usually given."

Ward whistled. "It wasn't a suicide, was it?"

"No, we'd have found the container and syringe if she injected herself with a dose that big. The victim wouldn't have had time to get rid of them. But we didn't find any drugs like that in the house, or supplies to administer it. You two look around the grounds and outbuildings."

"You think we'll find something out here?" Ward glanced around the yard.

"You never know. The killer might have tossed the syringe on his way out. Of course, you'll have to use proper procedure. Wear gloves, and tell me immediately if you find something."

"Sure." Ward threw Nate an eager glance. "We'd be happy to. Do you want us to bring you any chemicals we find?"

Blakeney hesitated. "We photographed the inside of the shed yesterday, but we didn't have time to go through it closely. You boys can have that detail. At this point, make note of anything poisonous, but the M.E.'s report seemed pretty conclusive that this was a pharmaceutical product." Blakeney stood with his arms folded across his chest.

He's in his element, Nate thought. Blakeney was putting on a real performance, as if he had a team of twenty or more men standing on the grass, when it was only Nate and his partner.

"List any rat poison, weed killer, fertilizer, anything like that. And if you should find any syringes or medical vials, report to me immediately. I'll be inside for a while. When I leave to do interviews, you can reach me on my cell." He gave them his personal phone number, and Nate felt that in itself was a small triumph.

Blakeney entered the house, letting the screen door slap to behind him.

"Do you want to take the garden shed?" Ward's eyes almost glittered.

"Sure," Nate said.

"Okay, I'll comb the flower beds and the yard."

The shed stood on the far edge of the lawn, opposite the woods, near an extension of the gravel driveway where Stella must have turned her car around hundreds of times. The door wasn't locked but simply secured with a small bolt through a hasp on the outside. Nate pulled on latex gloves, removed the bolt, and opened the door.

A small, dusty window did little more than define the location of the back wall. Nate stepped back and noted that no electric wires led to the shed. It figured. He headed back to his car.

Ward looked up from the flower beds. "Hey, did you find something already?"

"I'm getting a flashlight. It's really dark in there."

When he returned to the shed, he shined the flashlight beam around the dark corners and along the edges of the walls. He saw a broken down bicycle, a wooden barrel holding a couple of shovels and a rake, several sacks of mulch and potting soil, and various other gardening tools scattered over the workbench beneath the window. A couple of old bamboo fishing rods and a scythe hung from nails on the side wall. There was barely enough space among the junk to walk to the workbench.

They would have to go over the place with a fine-tooth comb. Nate stuck his head out the door again. "Hey, Ward, there's a lot of stuff in here. You want to give me a hand?"

Ward came to the shed door. "Wow. Let me get another flashlight."

They busied themselves sorting through the odds and ends, reading the label on every sack, bottle, bucket, and can they found. Nate made a meticulous list of each compound and its ingredients.

"There's a can of Off here," said Ward. "Did he say to report bug spray?"

Nate clenched his teeth and took the can from Ward, squinting at the fine print on the side. "We're not going to find anything useful, you know."

Ward grinned. "You're probably right. But we're still working on the murder investigation, not stopping little old ladies who forget to yield."

Nate set the can of insect repellant with several other items near the door and shined his flashlight under the bench. "Looks like that's about it." He checked his list over and joined Ward in the yard, searching carefully through the grass and flower beds.

A half hour later, Blakeney came out of the house and walked toward his cruiser. Nate took his list over and handed it to him.

"This is every chemical we found in the shed. No syringes or medicine bottles."

Blakeney scanned the paper and nodded. "Okay. When you're done out here, you can return to your regular detail. I'm off to do some interviews."

"You're sure you have time for this?" Emily

asked as she climbed into her car a short while later. "Because I don't want you complaining about how long it takes."

She hoped her little hint about work would get him to talk about that morning's investigation. She knew they were searching for the poison, but she hadn't heard if they had found anything, and she knew Nate wouldn't tell her if he was supposed to keep the information confidential.

"Me, complain?" Nate winked at her. "Nope, I'm well prepared for an extensive and exciting tuxedo-rental and pastel-napkin-buying adventure. Ward and I are going back on patrol at six tonight, so I'm yours until then."

Emily smiled. "Good. But first things first. Is Mr. Wolfe expecting us?" She'd have to content herself with anything new the lawyer had to tell them. Maybe the police hadn't found anything that morning after all.

"I called him last night," said Nate. "He said it would be fine if we wanted to come in this morning around ten."

"Then I guess we'd better hustle." Emily glanced at the clock on the dashboard. She hoped they would have enough time to accomplish several things on her to-do list before Nate went back to work that evening.

He started the car and they drove off.

"By the way," he said, "Blakeney agreed to take that cookie plate for analysis."

"Oh, good. I was hoping he would, but I was afraid he'd be mad at me for poking my nose where it doesn't belong again."

"I don't know, Em. I think he might have developed a bit of respect for you. You've certainly proved yourself helpful on several of his cases. And he hasn't called you Lois Lane in months."

Emily drew herself up. "Maybe I should change careers." She smiled smugly.

Nate laughed.

"Do you think we can stop in at the crime lab in Augusta on the way home?" She was very curious to find out who this Anthony Smithson was and if he had anything to do with Stella's death.

"I was hoping to stop in, anyway," said Nate. "I'll warn you, it may be too soon on the fingerprints. But we can ask if they've finished. And I'm hoping to learn more about the poison that killed Stella."

"What did you find out this morning?" Emily asked, since he seemed willing to discuss it.

Nate proceeded to tell her about the Procaine in Stella's system and searching the shed with Ward. "Of course, we didn't find anything out there. The big question is, how did all that stuff get into Stella's body? Apparently it's not something you would usually swallow. It's more of an IV drug, or an injection. Blakeney hoped we'd find a syringe or an empty container."

"Then I definitely think we should make time to stop at the crime lab," Emily said when he had finished. "Even if we don't finish my list. They will talk to you, won't they?"

"I think so."

"Maybe they'll explain how a person could poison a sweet, innocent woman with that stuff. Because it didn't look to me like there had been a struggle in her kitchen."

When they arrived at the attorney's office in Aswontee, John Wolfe's secretary showed them to his office. The lawyer had removed his suit jacket and loosened his tie. A stack of folders and papers lay on his desk.

"Come on in," said Wolfe. "Make yourselves comfortable."

"Thanks," said Nate. He and Emily sat in the burgundy leather chairs in front of Wolfe's desk. "Were you able to find out anything more about Stella Lessard's heirs?"

"As a matter of fact, yes," said Wolfe. "I have information that should shed some light on things."

Emily took out her slim reporter's notebook. "Do you mind if I note things down for the *Journal,* Mr. Wolfe?"

"Not at all," he replied. "Your coverage has been thorough but discreet."

"Have you been able to figure out if those two girls are telling the truth?" Nate asked. Emily smiled, knowing he was eager to get one or both of them off his hands and out of his hair.

"Not yet, unfortunately," said Wolfe. "And because I can't settle the estate until we determine who is the true heir, this process could go on for some time."

"Have you located Stella's daughter?" Emily asked.

"I'm fairly certain that Stella Lessard's daughter, known to us as Lois, is dead."

"I'm sorry to hear that." Several questions sprang into Emily's mind, but she decided to wait for Wolfe to tell the story in his own way.

"As you know, if one of those two girls can prove to be her daughter, she can inherit," the attorney said. "Otherwise —"

"Everything goes to Cedar." Nate frowned. "This is really crazy."

"Cedar?" Emily arched her eyebrows at Nate. "That might explain why he's so territorial about the house."

Nate shook his head slightly. "He was that way before he even knew he was an heir. I think it's a holdover from when she was alive. After Edgar died, Cedar felt like he was taking care of her. Cutting her firewood, fixing things around the house for her. He feels a sort of responsibility for the property."

"The situation is complex," Wolfe agreed. "There were documents in Mrs. Lessard's safe showing she had several certificates of deposit. I've notified the bank of her death. The heir stands to receive a sizable bequest in addition to the house. Oh, and she mentioned some jewelry in her will. We haven't found that yet."

"It wasn't in the safe?" Nate asked. "Ward and I brought you the jewelry box that was in her bedroom."

"The items she listed weren't in either, and I've found no indication that she had a safe deposit box." Wolfe opened a file folder and scanned the top sheet of paper. "I haven't received final word on either of the Williams girls' documents yet, but their birth certificates appear genuine."

"You said Stella's daughter is *known to us* as Lois," said Emily. She looked up from her notebook. "Did she have another name?"

"As a matter of fact, yes," said Wolfe. "I have a feeling that we may be very close to figuring out what's going on here. You see, at a certain point, Stella Lessard's child was placed in foster care. It seems that Stella and her husband were separated, though I haven't been able to find out exactly why this happened. It's very difficult to cut through the layers of red tape on sealed records."

Nate cleared his throat. "Well, sir, we know that Stella and her first husband were arrested for armed robbery about forty years ago. That's probably when their baby was placed in foster care."

Wolfe arched his eyebrows. "You've gained access to more information than I have. I was able to learn about the child's legal situation, but not why she went into state custody. Lois was only eighteen months old when she was removed from the home, and she was in foster care for about two years before she was adopted. When she was adopted, her new parents changed her name."

"To . . . ?" Emily could barely breathe as she waited for the revelation.

"Lois Pressey became Julia Bradley."

She sighed. "That's Jette's mother."

"And Jeanette's, too," said Nate. "Both

birth certificates list Nicholas Williams and Julia Bradley Williams as the parents."

"Now you see why we're still in the dark," said Wolfe. "According to their documents, they have the same parents. But they also have the same name. And that's highly suspicious."

"So one of them's an impostor," said Emily.

"More than likely," said Wolfe. "Probably one is the Williamses' real daughter, and the other somehow obtained a copy of her birth certificate. But we haven't figured out which is which."

"Sounds to me like they've both made pretty good cases," said Nate as they got back into the car.

Emily nodded. "But you know it's still possible they're both lying. If they had somehow found out the name Lois's adoptive parents gave her, they could have built false identities naming Julia Bradley as their mothers."

"But two of them?" Nate shook his head. "It's too crazy."

Emily buckled her seatbelt and sat back. "Maybe. I wonder why Stella's daughter had to go into foster care. Didn't she have any relatives to take care of the baby while she went to jail?"

"I don't know," said Nate. "A judge probably ruled on the case and declared Lois a ward of the state because both parents went to prison."

Emily frowned and stared out the window as they drove toward the highway. "I'm not an expert, but it seems to me that if there were grandparents or other relatives who could have helped, they would have gotten custody."

"We know Stella and her first husband split up after the burglary thing. Maybe they'd already argued over custody and who would take care of Lois. Maybe the state ruled that neither of them was a capable parent." Nate eased the car out onto the road. "I suppose it's possible that neither of them wanted her."

"But why? Everyone who knew Stella said she was a sweet, kind lady. Could she have changed that much over the years?"

"People do mellow," Nate said. "Maybe she didn't want kids when she was young. Maybe she'd thought about putting Lois up for adoption when she was born. Or maybe she figured that by the time she got out of jail her daughter was better off with her adoptive family than with a convicted criminal."

"That's a lot of maybes," said Emily. "The whole situation is fishy. But it should make a good story when it breaks wide open."

"That's for sure."

Half an hour later, they arrived at the formalwear rental shop. Nate parked the car in the only empty spot on the far end of the row. "Okay, so we agreed on pink suits, right?"

"Ha, ha." Emily let out a long sigh.

"Something wrong?"

"No. I just can't believe how fast time is going. I thought I'd be counting the days waiting for our wedding, but with everything that's been happening, I've almost been too busy to think about it."

"I know what you mean." Nate took her hand in his. "I'm sorry all this happened now."

"It's not your fault. But I am really glad you could take most of the day off so we could get some things done and spend some time together. Thanks for doing that."

"My pleasure." He leaned over to kiss her.

"You're going to get Gary and Jeff down here soon for their fittings, right?"

Nate raised his right hand. "I promise. It will be done."

She smiled. "Okay. Say, I almost forgot to tell you, I talked to Uncle Waldo last night.

He says he'll drive up with Mom for the wedding, and he'll be happy to walk me down the aisle. And he can stay overnight at the cottage with Mom and me the night before."

Nate brushed her hair back off her forehead. "I'm glad. I know you'll be missing your dad that day."

She nodded and pulled in a breath. "I've been thinking about Dad a lot lately. Having his brother there will help." She reached for the door handle. "Come on, let's go pick the style and get you measured. The sooner we get it over with, the sooner we can get back to crime busting."

"Mr. Wolfe said his next step would be to go down to Portland and interview Nicholas Williams. He should be able to tell us about his first wife and what happened to her, and if he really had any daughters named Jeanette."

Emily nodded. "I hope Wolfe is quick about it, because my patience is running a little thin. One way or another, I'm going to find out what happened to Lois Pressey."

When they arrived at the state police crime lab in Augusta at two o'clock, Nate and Emily entered the building and were shown to the desk of the officer compiling reports for the Lessard case.

"We've just completed the tests on the plate you brought in," Detective Wells said.

"Anything besides Emily's prints?" Nate asked.

Wells smiled at her. "I take it you're Emily Gray?"

"Yes, Officer. Pleased to meet you."

"She's my fiancée." Nate winked at her, and Wells chuckled.

"Congratulations. You did a good job of handling the evidence. We got a hit on the AFIS system from the fingerprints on the plate."

Emily beamed. "Fantastic!"

"Good thinking on getting the suspect's fingerprints that way," Wells said. "We got some very clear prints. And yours, of course, but that was all right. Miss Gray, your island visitor has a long record of convictions for domestic abuse, burglaries, armed robberies, and other crimes. And you were right. He *did* give you a false name."

"Who is he really?"

"Anton Pressey, more importantly known as Stella Lessard's first husband."

"You're kidding," said Nate.

Emily nodded. "I knew he was hiding something. It makes perfect sense."

"That isn't all. Pressey did time in the

Massachusetts State Prison for killing a man during an armed robbery years ago. His wife, Stella, opted to testify against him in exchange for a shorter sentence for herself."

"So, she was an accessory," said Nate. "That would explain why their child went into foster care."

"Precisely. We haven't followed up on the family, but you'll probably find there were no close relatives the judge deemed fit to take custody of the child. However, according to my research, Anton Pressey is free now and isn't wanted for any new crimes. He has a perfect right to visit Blue Heron Lake."

"But he arrived in Baxter around the time Stella died," said Emily. "Isn't that suspicious?"

"Sure it is," said the officer. "But it doesn't prove anything. You can be sure Detective Blakeney will check into his activities since he arrived in Baxter."

When they reached the car, Nate asked Emily to call the marina on her cell phone to find out exactly when Pressey arrived.

After she made the call, she turned to Nate with a troubled look on her face.

"So, what did Allison say?" he asked.

"Pressey arrived two days before Stella died."

13

Emily called the Maine State Archives on her cell phone as they drove out of the parking lot.

"Hello, do you have marriage records for the last . . . oh, say, twenty to fifty years?"

"No, ma'am," came the patient male voice. "You would go to the Office of Vital Statistics for that. Anything after 1922. The office is located at the Department of Human Services."

"Thank you." She closed her phone and smiled up at Nate. "Do we have time to run over to the Department of Human Services?"

Nate glanced at his watch. "If they don't make you wait too long."

"Great. It's over on State Street. I'll run in to the Office of Vital Statistics, and you can keep the engine running if you want."

"Oh, I'm not cutting it *that* close."

Thirty minutes later, the clerk handed her

the documents she had asked for, and Emily gladly paid the fee. She glanced at them, with Nate reading over her shoulder.

Nate whistled softly. "Having the right names paid big dividends."

"I'll say." Emily walked a few paces to an oak table and sank into a chair. In a whisper, she read the particulars to Nate. "Well, the marriage records aren't sealed, anyway. Stella was only seventeen when she married Anton Pressey."

"And if he got her mixed up in a robbery after they had Lois, her age goes a long way toward explaining why she never got her baby back," Nate said.

"Right. So that's Stella's first marriage. And then we have Julia Bradley's marriage to Nicholas Williams." Emily frowned down at the abstract.

"The Williams name is legit," Nate said.

"Yeah, but we pretty much figured it was, from the birth certificates. But I never expected to get these." She held up the last two documents.

Nate nodded. "Two girls with different first and middle names, born the same day to Julia and Nicholas Williams. The certificates Jette and Jeanette had looked identical, but they didn't say anything about twins. Since this is now a capital case, maybe Blakeney can get a warrant to unseal Lois's adoption records."

"And find out more about Jeanette and Jette." Emily glanced up at him. "It's so weird that they're both using the same name. Julia and Nicholas didn't name them both Jeanette."

"What was the second baby's name?" Nate asked.

"Marianne. One twin was Jeanette and the other was Marianne."

"Hey, maybe there are hospital records," Nate suggested.

"Good thinking. Suggest that to Blakeney. We need to get to the bottom of this. There were two Williams babies. If one of the girls who came to Baxter is the real Jeanette, the other could be trying to steal her identity to claim the estate."

"But where's the other one?" Nate asked. "Where's Baby Marianne now?"

Emily met his troubled gaze. "Good question." She snapped her fingers. "Divorce record. Why didn't I ask for it?"

"Whose, Stella's?"

"That might tell us something, but I was thinking more of Lois's, or should I say Julia's? Jette and Jeanette both told us that Nicholas and Julia Williams divorced."

"Would they put information about the

children on the divorce decree?" Nate asked.

"Yes. We get them for the newspaper, but we don't publish the part about custody decisions, to protect the kids' privacy. But it should be on the abstract."

"Let's ask for it, then."

Fifteen minutes later, they rushed out to Emily's car.

"Now you *will* be late," she said as he unlocked the passenger door for her.

"Ward will understand when I tell him what kept us."

Emily buckled her seatbelt and thumbed through the papers again as Nate headed the car up Western Avenue, toward the interstate highway. "Twin girls, and when they divorced, the parents each got custody of one child."

"Which parent got which baby?" Nate asked.

"The father got Jeanette, and the mother got Marianne."

Nate frowned. "Then Jette's the impostor."

"Not necessarily. We've got to keep an open mind."

Nate chuckled and shook his head. "At least you assume we're 'of one mind.' "

Emily shrugged. "You know what I mean. I'm just saying, we haven't proven anything except that there were actually two girls born to these parents nineteen years ago. We haven't proven that the two up in Baxter are the twins."

"Yeah, that's right. They don't even look alike."

"Oh, I don't know." Emily cocked her head toward her shoulder and tried to picture the two Williams girls. "Their eyes are the same color, and they have roughly the same build. Who's to say what color Jette's hair was originally?"

The next morning, Blakeney arrived at the marina house at nine thirty, while Nate was mowing his scrap of a lawn.

"Where's Miss Gray this morning?" he asked when Nate had shut off the mower.

"At the newspaper office." Nate hoped Blakeney's sober expression didn't bode ill for Emily.

"At least she's not out on the island. Come on, let's go over to the office. I don't want to have to tell this twice, and I think Miss Gray deserves to hear it firsthand."

Nate climbed into Blakeney's patrol car and rode the short distance down the street with him.

Emily and Felicia sat at their desks when the men entered. Emily was typing industriously but left off as soon as she saw them. Felicia hastily ended a telephone conversation.

"Good morning, ladies."

Emily jumped up. "Detective Blakeney, how nice of you to visit us."

"Instead of making you chase me all over the county for an update?" Blakeney actually smiled as she wheeled Charlie's empty chair over for him. Nate claimed the one visitor's chair in the cramped office, and they all sat down.

"This is an honor, Detective," Felicia said. "I take it you have some news for our humble publication?"

"Oh, yeah, plenty of news. When's your next edition?"

"Tomorrow. I'll send it to the printer in a couple of hours. Please tell me there's a reason for us to remake page 1. Something more exciting than the fishing derby rules."

"I'm sure Jeff Lewis and the staff at the lodge won't mind if we bump the fishing derby advance to page 3," Emily said eagerly.

Blakeney sighed and rested his hat on his knee. "I've got to hand it to you, Miss Gray. I tried to dig up records on Stella Lessard's daughter, and so did John Wolfe. But we were looking for the wrong names. Without the fingerprints you and Nate brought me, it probably would have taken a long time to make the connection to Anton Pressey. And now you've discovered that Lois — that is, Julia Bradley — had twins."

"I just worked backward on that, using the names Jeanette and Jette Williams gave us," Emily said. "I figured if I couldn't get at Lois through her mother, I'd go at her through her daughter, or as it turned out, her daughters."

Blakeney held her gaze. "Good work. I took your suggestion and had a cozy chat with the detective sergeant at the Portland Police Department last night. It was touch and go, but their chief paid attention and found a judge who agreed to issue a warrant for the hospital records."

Nate, Emily, and Felicia waited, barely breathing.

"One of those babies, Marianne Williams, was born with a birth defect."

Emily caught her breath. "She's the one the mother gained custody of."

Blakeney nodded. "She had a heart condition. An opening between the chambers of the heart. According to the doctor's opinion at the time, her condition might lead to further health problems, and possibly require expensive care or surgery. Or it might heal itself as the baby grew older."

"So . . ." Emily jotted something on her notepad. "What happened to Marianne? Did she survive?"

"We don't know yet. One of our best researchers is trying to track down a death certificate as we speak. If he doesn't find one, we'll have to assume Marianne Williams is alive."

"But . . ." Emily fell silent, studying her notepad.

"Detective Blakeney," Nate said, "do you think one of the claimants to the estate is Marianne Williams?"

"Maybe. But then, why isn't she using her real name?"

"I have a theory."

Blakeney arched his eyebrows. "Want to share it?"

Nate inhaled deeply and glanced at Emily. She gave him an encouraging smile, and he nodded. "I've been thinking all along that maybe one of these girls assumed the identity of Stella's granddaughter in an attempt to claim the estate. I don't know how she knew about the relationship or any of that, but . . ."

Felicia nodded vigorously. "If the baby named Marianne died, someone else could try to step into her place."

"Then why not claim to be Marianne Williams, not Jeanette?" Blakeney shook his head.

Emily tapped the end of her pen against the notepad. "Think about this, sir. Nicholas and Julia Williams divorced when those twins were only a few months old. What if neither of them wanted the 'sick' child? What if they both wanted the healthier infant, Jeanette?"

"But there was only one healthy baby, and only one Jeanette."

Nate slowly raised his head as a memory tugged at his mind. "Jeanette — that is, the girl claiming to be Jeanette — the one who grew up in Nicholas Williams's family —"

"What about her?" Blakeney asked.

"She told me the other day that she had a heart murmur. It kept her out of the military when she wanted to enlist. She hadn't known anything about it until she went for the physical."

Emily's face cleared. "That's believable. If the mother *said* she was giving her ex the healthy baby, but really she gave him the one with the heart condition, she would know that the baby she raised was really Jeanette, and chances are, she would call her Jeanette, because that was her real name. Meanwhile, the father raised Marianne *thinking* she was Jeanette and calling her Jeanette. He even had a copy of Jeanette's birth certificate to 'prove' it."

Blakeney scratched his chin. "So . . . you're thinking the Marianne twin survived and grew up using the name Jeanette."

"It would explain everything." Emily looked from him to Nate, her eyes bright with excitement.

Nate hated to burst the balloon of her somewhat plausible theory. "But, Em, if Nicholas got the sick baby, wouldn't he know it?"

"Not necessarily. He and Julia were probably separated for a while before the divorce became final. I'm guessing Julia had both girls to herself for several weeks, maybe even months."

"They're not identical," Felicia pointed out.

"Not now," Emily said. "But how do we know how much they looked alike at two or three months? And besides, if Julia only took one child along when she delivered Marianne to Nicholas, and he didn't see the twins together . . ."

Felicia nodded in agreement. "And if Marianne had been progressing and was looking and acting a little healthier . . ."

"That's an insult to men in general," Nate

protested. "To say he wouldn't know his own children."

Emily shrugged, holding her palms up. "I did a story once on three sets of twins in the same elementary school in Connecticut. One of their mothers admitted that even when her boys were six years old, she had trouble telling them apart now and then."

Blakeney eyed her thoughtfully. "And if, as you say, the father didn't have access to the babies for a while, until the judge ruled on the custody question . . . Babies do change fast at that age. Miss Gray, I think that's a credible theory you've got there."

Emily grinned. "Thank you. Would you like some coffee, Detective?"

"Oh, no, thanks. I need to interview the two Misses Williams again. Of course, I won't advance this hypothesis of yours to them at this point. I wouldn't want to raise their expectations until we get some proof. And I still plan to drive down and talk face-to-face with the father, Nicholas Williams, but that will kill half a day." He nodded and stood up. "Lots of leads to chase down. I wonder if the hospital made footprints of the babies when they were born." He headed for the door. "Of course, first I'm going to pay a visit to Anton Pressey. I suppose I'll have to rent a boat."

"He hasn't left the island all week, as far as we know," Nate told him.

"Oh, Detective!" Emily jumped up and followed Blakeney across the room. "How much of this can we put in tomorrow's *Journal*?"

He hesitated. "Nothing about Pressey. There's not much there yet, and I don't want to spook him. I guess it's safe to say we've discovered Lois's name change and verified that she gave birth to twins. I'm going to break that news to the two girls right now. But no speculating on whether either of these girls is a true heir, or on what happened to either baby. I could get into all kinds of hot water if it got around that I've been wondering if that Marianne baby died and the custodial parent somehow found a 'replacement.' "

"Oh, we won't go into that," Emily assured him. "Facts only. Thank you, sir."

He nodded. "We're close to breaking this case. You can quote me on that, Emily."

Emily's jaw dropped as Blakeney went out and closed the door. "Did you hear that? He called me Emily!"

"Told you he likes you now." Nate smiled at her.

"So what do we do with all this information?" Felicia wailed. "We have to sit on ninety percent of it."

"We make hay with the other ten percent." Emily sat down at her computer.

"You write the story on Stella's daughter," Felicia said. "I'll type in a brief about the murder and use Blakeney's quote."

"Got it." Emily opened a new document.

Felicia's phone rang and she grabbed the receiver. "*Baxter Journal.*"

Nate leaned down and kissed Emily's cheek. "Something tells me I should let you two work while I finish mowing my lawn before my shift starts."

He stepped out onto the sidewalk as Blakeney was getting into his car. Nate nodded and turned toward home. Cedar Sproul, his stringy hair tousled and his eyes wild, hurried down the sidewalk toward him.

"Cedar! What brings you here?"

"I saw the cop car." Cedar panted as he nodded toward Blakeney's vehicle.

The detective spotted him just as he was about to shut his door and got out of the car again. "What can we do for you, Mr. Sproul?"

"Someone's in Stella's house. They broke the tape down."

Nate shot a glance at Blakeney.

"You saw someone go in Mrs. Lessard's house?" The detective came up onto the sidewalk to stand beside them.

"No. There's a car there, and the tape is down. The door's open."

"Did you go in?" Nate asked sternly.

"No. I went to the marina to get you, but you weren't there. Then I saw the cop car down here."

Blakeney clapped him on the shoulder. "You did the right thing. Thanks. We'll check it out." He glanced at Nate's grass-stained jeans and T-shirt. "Feel like backing me up, Holman? No time to get into uniform."

"Sure." Nate jumped into the passenger seat, and Blakeney headed out of town toward the road that wound about the southern end of Blue Heron Lake.

"Probably it's the lawyer," Blakeney said, "but we have to make sure."

When they reached Stella's house, a maroon Toyota was sitting in the driveway. Blakeney parked his cruiser squarely behind it, effectively blocking the exit, and punched the license number into the computer on his dashboard. He studied the results and grunted.

Nate raised his eyebrows but said nothing.

Blakeney opened his door. "Come on."

At that moment, a plump, balding man

Nate had never seen before came out onto the porch of the little house holding a fishing rod. Nate got out of the car and followed as Blakeney strode toward the man.

"Wilbur Lessard?"

The man gulped. "That's me."

"What are you doing here?"

"I came to get something that belongs to me."

"I'll have to charge you with breaking and entering."

"I have a key."

Blakeney scowled at him. "This is a crime scene and was marked as such. Crossing the police line is a crime. So is theft." He looked pointedly at the fishing rod.

"Hey, I'm not stealing anything," Lessard said. "Stella told me a couple of months ago she'd give me all my brother's fishing equipment. Don't know why she didn't give it to me years ago, but she didn't. Anyway, the season's open and I wanted my gear. I figured if I waited for that lawyer to settle things, I'd never get it."

"I don't believe you were named in Stella Lessard's will," Blakeney said.

"So? She promised me."

"Nevertheless, sir, if she died without delivering the goods to you, I believe it's now part of her estate. You'll have to check with her attorney to be certain, but in the meantime, I suggest you put that rod and anything else you've removed from the house back immediately, or I'll charge you with theft, in addition to trespass and entering a crime scene without authorization."

Wilbur Lessard's jaw dropped. "I didn't do anything."

Blakeney stared at him. "What part of my instructions did you not understand?"

Lessard backed up a few steps into the house and emerged again minus the fishing rod.

"Anything else?" Blakeney asked. "Did you put anything in your car?"

"No."

"Let's take a look." Blakeney followed Lessard to his car. After a quick look into the passenger compartment and the trunk, he said sternly, "All right, then, I'll just warn you. You have no right to be on this property. If I find out you've been here again, or that you've taken anything from the property, you'll be in the county jail faster than you can say 'fly casting,' you understand?"

Lessard nodded and blinked at Nate.

"I'll take the key," Blakeney said. "If you are named heir to the estate, the attorney will give it back to you at the proper time." He held out his hand.

Wilbur slowly reached into his pocket and took out a key ring. Blakeney stood like a statue of a storm trooper while the older man fumbled to remove a single key from the ring. At last he got it free and placed it in the detective's hand.

"All right, get in your vehicle." Blakeney passed him and went into the house.

Wilbur came slowly down the steps and squeezed up his face. "She promised me that stuff. Isn't that a verbal contract?"

Nate cleared his throat and glanced toward the open doorway. "I don't know, sir. Perhaps you can call Mr. Wolfe and ask him. He would know about things like that."

"Yeah. Right." Wilbur walked toward his car.

Nate wondered if he should go around to Cedar's house later and warn him again to stay away from the crime scene. But if he hadn't been there today, they might not have known about Wilbur Lessard's escapade. He decided to let the matter drop unless someone complained about Cedar again.

Blakeney came out and locked the door. He stooped and picked up the loose end of the yellow crime scene tape, looked at it, and sighed. "I'll have to fix this, but I'd better move the car first so the chump can leave."

14

"Hey, isn't that Jeanette?" Nate pulled his sunglasses off and stared across the water.

Emily followed his gaze. Beyond the Vigues' dock, the newly arrived Kimmel boys were swimming and jumping off the float anchored offshore from their parents' cottage. A shapely young woman in a black maillot suit climbed the ladder to the float, and Rocky Vigue floated nearby, laughing and splashing water at the boys.

"Yes," she said. "Apparently Rocky went over to the lodge and asked her out again, and this time she accepted. Truly came by this morning, all flustered, and told me. She and Marvin couldn't believe Rocky asked if he could bring a girl out here for lunch and a swim."

"Well, all right." Nate pushed the glasses back on. "Good for Jeanette. She just went up a notch in my book."

Rocky's father, Marvin, was lighting the

gas grill on the flat speck of lawn above the Vigues' dock. Nate waved, and Marvin waved back with his lighter.

"Morning, Nate," he called. "You're not working today?"

"I'll be patrolling this afternoon and evening."

Marvin nodded. "You and Emily are welcome to chow down with us."

"Thanks, Marvin." Nate shot a glance at Emily.

She shrugged and asked softly, "You want to?"

"Why not?"

She nodded and called, "How about if we throw our hot dogs on your grill later?"

"Sure thing, Emily. Any time." Marvin closed the lid on his grill and ambled toward his cottage whistling.

"It should be interesting to get Jeanette's take on all that's happened the last couple of days," Nate said.

Emily eyed the young people in the water and looked back at Nate. He always hung back when the water was cold. Even though she knew Nate was wearing his swimsuit under his jeans, he probably hadn't made up his mind that he wanted to swim yet. Blue Heron Lake was still chilly, although the bright sun had warmed the water several degrees over the last few days. It was warm enough that Raven and her staffers had been out water skiing that morning.

Emily's mind flitted back to the case and the revelations about Stella's past. "Did Blakeney get around to interviewing Pressey yesterday?"

"He did. Last night he caught up with Ward and me about suppertime. He told Pressey that the authorities know who he is. Pressey said he used a false name to rent the cottage because he didn't want to embarrass Stella. He came here hoping to talk to her, but if she didn't want to see him, he didn't see any reason to let her neighbors know about it."

"Oh, how thoughtful." Emily grimaced at him.

Nate leaned back in his lawn chair and crossed his ankles. "He admitted being in town before Stella died, but he told Blakeney he hadn't worked up his nerve to approach her yet. Then he heard she'd died and decided to just spend a quiet week on the island. He had hoped to reconcile, but he was too late."

"Why am I not convinced?" Emily stared at the glassy lake. Pressey was up to no good. She was sure of it.

"If he killed her, wouldn't he have gotten

out of town before anyone knew who he was?" Nate asked. He watched her closely. Emily could always tell when he expected her to say something brilliant, but she didn't have an explanation for Anton Pressey's actions.

"What do you say we go over and say hi to Jeanette?" She jumped up from her chair before Nate could answer and picked up the clean towels from the edge of the dock.

Nate followed her over to the Kimmels' wharf. Emily laid the folded towels down and dropped her flip-flops and terry cover-up neatly on top, feeling a little self-conscious in her red and white one-piece suit.

"Race you to the float."

"No fair. I'm not ready." Nate hurried to fling off his T-shirt, glasses, watch, and sneakers. Emily dived off the dock before he was down to his swim trunks. She struck out for the float and was halfway there before she heard the splash behind her as he dove in.

He caught up as Emily climbed the ladder. Jeanette was sitting on the float watching Rocky and the three Kimmel boys. Stevie, the oldest, was egging on his brothers to help him duck Rocky.

"Hi, Jeanette. Nice day, isn't it?" Emily

sat down on the canvas-covered deck of the float near Jeanette.

"Yes. The water's a little cold, but the sun feels great."

Nate climbed up and smiled at her. "Hi. How are you doing?"

Jeanette hesitated. "I admit I'm a little off balance right now. I suppose you know about my mother, Officer Holman. That is, my birthmother. Detective Blakeney told me yesterday that Julia Bradley and Lois Pressey were the same person."

"Yes, he reported on his findings to the sheriff's department. And please call me Nate."

Jeanette pursed her lips. "I'm at a loss as to what I should feel now."

"What do you mean?" Emily asked.

"The detective says my mother gave birth to twins, and . . . we were separated." Jeanette swiveled her head and stared at Emily. "Does this mean that punk girl is my sister?"

Emily reached out and touched Jeanette's arm lightly. "We don't know. I'm sure the authorities will sort it out soon."

Jeanette shook her head. "I don't want to be related to her." She drew her knees up and hugged them, resting her head on her arms.

Nate looked helplessly at Emily, but she couldn't offer him more than a weak smile. He turned his attention to Rocky and the boys, who were getting wilder and noisier by the minute.

"Help, Nate!" Rocky yelled. "These kids are going to drown me."

Stevie and his brothers laughed and jumped on Rocky, but he was so buoyant they couldn't drag him under.

"You know," Jeanette said, "even when my dad told me about my . . . my real mother . . . he never mentioned a sister." She wiped her glistening eyes with the back of her hand. "He said my mother was dead. And I guess that's true." She shrugged. "How do I know what to believe?"

"Have you called your father since you got here?" Emily asked.

Jeanette shook her head. "I called and told Mom — my stepmother — that I got here okay, but Dad was at work. I'm sort of afraid to talk to him. He lied to me all these years." Her brown eyes narrowed. "When he finally told me about her, he said he'd seen a news story about a woman with the name of my maternal grandmother. I found an obituary online for Stella Lessard, and I knew I had to come to Baxter to see if I could learn more about my grandmother and that part of my family. But I was pretty upset with my dad when I left. He could have told me about her when she was alive. I just don't know if I'm ready to talk to him yet or not."

Emily nodded. "I'm sorry it all came out this way. You've had a tough time."

Jeanette's mouth hardened into a firm line, and she drew in a deep breath. "I just won't believe that Jette, or whatever her name really is, and I could be twins."

Emily felt tears sting her own eyes. She tried to smile, but her lips wobbled. She hated losing control, but whenever she was reminded of her own dear father and the miserable excuse for a stepfather she'd gotten after Wiley Gray died, she teared up. She cleared her throat. "You know, it's possible Jette also heard the news story about her grandmother and had feelings similar to yours. Only she didn't have a dad and a stepmom or brothers and sisters. She was all alone."

Jeanette tossed her head, shaking water droplets from her hair. "More likely she heard the newscasts about the missing heir and made up her relationship to Grandmother."

Emily looked up at Nate, pleading silently for his help.

Nate knelt beside them and said gently, "Detective Blakeney is hoping to speak to your father today."

"He told me," Jeanette said.

"Well, maybe that will help uncover what really happened. I don't know if Jette is telling the truth or not, but if she is, then you two could be sisters, and in that case, you'd both be heirs to Stella's estate."

Jeanette held his gaze for a long moment. "Would it still help you to do that DNA test?"

Emily caught her breath. Was this the answer to her earlier prayers?

Nate nodded slowly. "Yes, it would. That would be the proof, and I think it would give you both peace of mind."

Jeanette looked past him, toward the faraway mainland. "I only refused when you asked because . . . because I knew I didn't have proof that Stella was my grandmother. I only had my dad's word on that, and he'd lied to me. I didn't want to find out this was another lie. But now . . ." She faced Nate again. "I'd like to take the test."

"That's terrific. Thanks." Nate smiled at her and glanced at Emily. Tears streamed down Emily's cheeks, and she sniffed.

Jeanette rolled over to her knees and

stood. "Let's not get weepy about it. I'm sure now that I am Stella Lessard's flesh and blood. I don't need the test for that. But I want to prove that I'm not Jette's sister."

After lunch, Jeanette excused herself and headed her boat back toward Lakeview Lodge. Rocky stood on his father's dock watching her mournfully.

"Guess I'd better get going, too," Nate said. "Em, are you coming over to town, or do you want to stay here this afternoon?"

"I'll go over and see how Felicia's doing."

Nate nodded and picked up his towel. Emily usually had Friday off, since that was one of the *Journal*'s publication days. Then she spent most of Saturday and Monday preparing for the Tuesday edition. But everyone's schedule was out of whack since Stella's death had been ruled a murder.

When they reached the marina house, Emily frowned as she climbed onto his dock.

"What's the matter?" Nate asked. "Besides everything, I mean."

She cracked a smile. "Just thinking about Anton Pressey. Don't you think Blakeney should at least take him in for questioning?"

"He talked to him, but they can't place him at the scene of the crime. For instance, they didn't find any of his fingerprints at Stella's house. We asked Cedar, and he didn't remember seeing anyone like Pressey at Stella's."

"Maybe he didn't do it at her house."

"What do you mean?"

"Maybe he poisoned her somehow in another place, but it didn't take effect until after she was home."

Nate sighed. "I don't pretend to know about things like that, but Detective Blakeney did say it's a fast-acting drug. That's one reason the M.E. didn't rule it a suicide. The paraphernalia would have been found near the body."

Emily whipped around to face him. "What about the girls? Allison told me Jon's been taking the *Journal* out to Anton Pressey with his groceries. If you were Pressey and two young women who were supposedly granddaughters you'd never met were a mile away, wouldn't you want to meet them?"

Nate walked slowly beside her to the back door of his house. "Yeah. Maybe. I don't know. He could be waiting to let the authorities decide if they really are Lois's kids. Or maybe he hasn't put it all together yet."

Emily shivered.

"What are you thinking?" He eyed her closely.

"Jette. Suppose she did go to see him the other day, when Raven saw her in the boat? Did you ever ask her about that?"

"Yeah. She said she was just out exploring the lake."

Emily shook her head, obviously dissatisfied. "He's a hardened criminal."

"Yeah. Just the type of man those girls don't need in their lives. Come on. I'll put this stuff inside and walk you over to the office. Then I'd better get ready for work."

As they walked hand in hand along the sidewalk, Emily was quiet, and he knew she was stewing over Anton Pressey.

"Look, Em, there's not much I can do about the situation until Blakeney has enough evidence to make a move. Finding out how Stella was poisoned is critical. That will help us find out who did it."

Emily stopped walking and jerked her chin toward the Heron's Nest. "Looks like Jette's going somewhere."

Nate looked toward the driveway of the bed-and-breakfast. Jette was swinging a backpack onto the passenger seat of her car. She'd changed her black nail polish and lipstick for a garish purple today.

"Maybe just going for a hike," Nate said.

Emily tugged him toward the driveway. "Hi, Jette!"

She turned and looked at them. An expression Nate couldn't interpret flickered across her face before her bright smile broke through.

"Hello, newspaper girl. Where's your uniform, Boy Scout?"

Nate laughed. "Hanging in the closet. Where are you off to this afternoon?"

"Oh, just poking around. Detective Blakeney says I need to hang loose for a couple more days. Thought I'd see what they do for fun in Aswontee. I already found out they roll up the sidewalks in Baxter at five o'clock."

Emily stepped closer to her, and Nate gave an inward sigh. He didn't really feel like talking to Goth girl just now.

"You should have come out to the island this morning," Emily said. "We went swimming and had a barbecue with our neighbors, the Vigues and the Kimmels." Nate noticed that she didn't mention Jeanette's presence.

"Sounds like fun," Jette said. "Maybe next time."

"Yeah. Hey, my friend Raven said she saw you near the island in a boat Tuesday. You didn't happen to go visit the man in the cottage on the end, did you?"

Jette licked her lips and glanced at Nate,

then back to Emily. "I was just out exploring."

"Oh, good. Because he's not the nice old guy some people think he is. The police have found out he's an ex-con."

"Really?"

"Yeah."

Nate touched Emily's shoulder. When she glanced up at him, he raised his eyebrows. *What are you doing, Em?*

Jette looked down at her ergonomic sandals. Behind her makeup, her face had gone pink. Emily snapped her eyes toward Jette's car. Nate frowned, trying to understand what she was getting at. He looked at the small, dark green car. Suddenly it hit him. Through the back window he glimpsed a suitcase and two smaller bags.

"You're not getting ready to leave town, are you, Jette?" he asked.

She inhaled carefully. "Okay, it's too weird. I just want to go home and get back to normal. The lawyer can call me if I need to come back up here."

"Does this have to do with Anton Pressey?" Nate asked.

She pressed her purple lips together then squared her shoulders. "He's my grandfather."

"Yes, if you're really Stella's granddaughter."

She nodded, her eyes not quite meeting his.

"How did you know he was on the island, Jette? Did you meet him before you came to Baxter?"

Emily kept quiet and let Nate ask the questions now, but he could feel her excited energy as she waited with him for Jette's answer.

"Look, I could have said I never heard of him in my life, but that would be a lie." Jette ran a hand through her short hair, standing it up in an even wilder pattern than usual. "He looked my mom up a couple of years ago. He'd been in jail for a long time, and Mom was kind of scared of him. She hadn't seen him since she was, like, a year and a half old." Jette shook her head, and Nate saw the glitter of tears in her eyes. "She had cancer by then. She didn't need another distraction in her life, and when he called, she refused to see him."

"So she didn't reconcile with him at all?" Nate asked.

"No. She told him to leave us alone. And he did, so far as I could tell. Mom had her chemotherapy and everything, but . . . it wasn't enough."

The tears overflowed her eyelids and trickled down her cheeks. Emily stepped closer and put her arm around Jette's shoulders. "That was a really rough time for you."

Jette nodded and sniffled. "When she died, I felt so alone." She blinked and swatted at a tear. "He showed up at her funeral."

That surprised Nate. "How about Stella? Was she there, too?"

Jette shook her head. "So far as I know, she never even tried to find Mom. I didn't know much about her. I didn't even know she'd been in jail, too, until after I met Grandpa." She stared at Nate, the old defiance cropping up again. "Yes, I agreed to see him after the funeral. I got to know him a little bit. He admitted he was a lousy husband and father. He was so . . . apologetic for not being part of my life and for letting the whole family down, that I decided it would be nice to have a grandpa. To have *somebody* again."

Emily rubbed Jette's shoulder. "I can't say I blame you, Jette. He is your family, but . . . well, you know he did some very bad things."

Jette glared at her and stepped away. "He's paid for all his crimes. He's a free man now, and he shouldn't be treated like a leper."

"You and your grandfather got close?" Nate asked.

"Kind of. We didn't have any memories or traditions, so we made some of our own. He got an apartment in Portsmouth, and we'd do things together on the weekend."

"And you knew when he came to Baxter?"

Jette winced. "Well, I . . ." She sighed and let her head droop. "Okay, yes. He told me he was going out of town for a few days, but he didn't tell me why. I didn't think much about it. But then he called me and asked me to drive up here. He said my grandmother had died, and he wanted to see me. He met me in Bangor and told me about the will and everything. He said I was the missing heir, since Mom had died, and I should make an appointment with the lawyer. But he asked me not to tell anyone he was here. He didn't want to complicate things, but he said he'd stick around and keep a low profile, in case I needed him." She looked at Nate and then Emily, her chin set with determination. "He's been nothing but good to me."

Nate nodded. "I don't doubt it. I'm sorry I upset you, but I think Detective Blakeney needs to know about this. You see, Anton Pressey was here in Baxter before Stella died."

"You don't —" Her dark eyes narrowed. "Grandpa didn't do anything to her."

"Then who did?"

Jette said nothing, but her lower lip trembled, setting her lip ring aquiver.

"Just take your bags back inside, Jette," Nate said gently. "You need to stay here."

Jette sighed and yanked the backpack out of the car.

"Come on, I'll help you," Emily said. "Detective Blakeney will straighten this all out, but you need to be where he can reach you easily until that happens."

Nate watched the two young women go into the Heron's Nest carrying Jette's luggage. He exhaled deeply and took out his cell phone.

"Detective Blakeney? This is Deputy Holman. I just learned that Jette Williams has been in contact with her alleged grandfather — that is, with Anton Pressey — for the last two years. She did visit him on Grand Cat Tuesday, and he's the one who encouraged her to come to Baxter and claim the Lessard estate. She was going to leave town, but I think I've convinced her that would be a bad idea."

"Oh, great," Blakeney responded. "You couldn't discover this when I was in Baxter? You know I'm in Portland, don't you?"

Nate swallowed hard. "Yes, sir, you did say you were going to question Nicholas Williams today. I'm sorry it's inconvenient, but Emily and I found out sort of by accident that Jette was packing her things and planning to skip town."

"All right, all right. It's a good thing you were there, I guess. But there's no way I can get up there for another three hours. I may as well wait until tomorrow morning."

"Uh, sir, if you think it's appropriate, I could bring Pressey in for questioning. Now that we know he was in contact with one of the girls, shouldn't we . . ." He wanted to say "interrogate him," but he was afraid Blakeney would jump all over him. Even long distance, the prospect didn't appeal to him.

"I wouldn't want you to talk to him alone, Holman. He may be getting on in years, but he's done a lot of jail time. You don't have the experience to deal with a man like that by yourself. They're crafty."

Nate wished he could say Ward Delaney would be with him, but for the first time he was scheduled to patrol alone that evening while Ward had a night off for his daughter's graduation. "Well, sir, I really think Pressey's a flight risk."

"If you feel it's so urgent that you have to

do it today, I'll send you a state trooper for backup. You wait until he gets there, you hear me?"

"Yes, sir." Nate couldn't help smiling grimly. Blakeney seemed sure he would bungle the job.

"You may as well hear it from me: The medical examiner found a tiny puncture wound on the victim's back. That about nails it — the killer stuck her with a fine needle from behind. The M.E. says that dose of Procaine would work so fast, she probably never knew what happened."

Nate swallowed hard again, thinking about Stella Lessard stirring her spaghetti sauce while a killer sneaked up behind her with a lethal syringe.

"So watch yourself, Holman. Don't take any chances."

"No, sir." Nate hesitated then said, "It did cross my mind that Pressey and Jette Williams might have arranged to leave Baxter together. I think we should question him as soon as possible."

"Okay. I'll go along with you and call the barracks for backup. But it will probably take the unit awhile to get out there."

"Thank you, sir." As Nate hung up, Emily emerged from the Heron's Nest. "Is Jette staying put for sure?" he asked.

"I think so. Any reason to believe otherwise?"

Nate shrugged. "I wonder if she's talked to 'Grandpa' today."

"She didn't mention it, and you know he can't get phone service on the island." Emily glanced at her watch. "I'd better see if Felicia needs me."

"Right," Nate said. "And I'd better go home and get into uniform."

He hurriedly dressed for work and glanced out his front window to see if the trooper had arrived yet. Instead he saw Emily sauntering up the front steps. He opened the door.

"Hey. What's up?"

"Felicia says she's all set for today. She's heading for a Chamber of Commerce meeting, but I can goof off. Imagine that!"

"Yeah, sounds good." Nate hesitated. Should he tell her what he was going to do as soon as the backup arrived? "Uh, Em . . ."

"What?"

"I want you to go straight home, okay? To the cottage, I mean."

"That's what I plan to do." She eyed him suspiciously. "What's going on?"

"Nothing."

"Oh, yes, something is. You've got that shifty look in your eyes. You can't evade the question with me, Nathan Pierce Holman."

He chuckled. "You got me. Blakeney's sending a state trooper, and we're going out to the island and question Pressey. We may even take him to the sheriff's office for questioning."

"Wow. Based on what Jette told us?"

"Yes. He got her to come up here. Who knows what else he hasn't told us?"

"Good point." She looked up at him hopefully. "How about if I —"

"No, Em. I want you to go home and stay there. Or go visit with my mom if you want. But I don't want you anywhere nearby when we talk to Anton Pressey."

Her face went sober and she nodded. "Okay. For you, I'll do it." She stretched up on tiptoe and kissed him. "I guess I'll go back to the island. Let me know what happens, okay?"

"Sure." Nate turned her toward the back deck and slid his arm around her waist. "Come on. I'll see you to your boat. Which reminds me, I'm really proud of you. You almost handle that motor like a pro now."

She set out for Grand Cat with a cheerful wave, and Nate stood watching until he could barely see her boat, heading for the north end of the island. His phone whirred, and he reached for it with a sigh.

"Deputy Holman."

"Nate, this is Gary. Detective Blakeney told me to come help you out with a sticky interview."

Nate grinned. "All right! I'm glad it's you."

"I'll be there in ten minutes," Gary said.

15

Nate laid the cabin cruiser neatly alongside the dock at Derbin's cottage, exactly right, just the way he'd done for almost twenty years.

Gary grinned at him. "You shoulda been a pilot, Nate. Three-point landing every time."

"Thanks." Nate ran his finger around the neckline of his Kevlar vest. It was nearly suppertime, but the direct sun on the lake warmed him thoroughly, and the extra layer of the vest made him sweat. It hadn't surprised him to see the Kimmel boys splashing about their float again, farther up the island shore.

Gary tied the boat up, and they both climbed onto the dock.

"You do the talking," Gary said as they walked up to the cottage.

Nate's knock brought no response.

"He was outside the other day, when Emily and I came." He turned and peered down the rocky shore.

"Let's take a look around."

Gary stepped down off the porch, but Nate stood still, gazing down the path toward the dock and his boat.

"Hey."

"Yeah?" Gary turned and looked up at him.

"His boat's gone. We should have realized it when we docked. He rented a boat at the marina to use while he's here."

"Maybe he's out fishing."

Nate decided to save time and turned the doorknob. The door swung open.

"Pressey?" he yelled into the kitchen.

Gary looked at him, his eyebrows arched.

Nate frowned and called again, "Pressey? It's Nate Holman. Are you in there?"

Silence greeted him.

"I'm going in." Nate drew his pistol.

"Don't you —"

Nate ignored his cousin and stepped forward. He felt a little silly, entering the empty kitchen in the alert stance and peering all around at every possible place of concealment. If anyone fussed about him entering the cottage without an invitation, Nate could remind them of the Henry Derbin incident and claim he was worried about the renter. A mug, bowl, and spoon rested on the tiny countertop beside the sink, but they were the only signs that someone had been there recently. He heard Gary in the doorway behind him.

"Clear!" Nate moved on to the living room door. Again, nothing. Everything looked as though no one had disturbed it for weeks. He saw no personal items lying about. He knew the layout of the single-story cottage from his past visits to Mr. Derbin, and he checked the bathroom next, pushing back the shower curtain. When he emerged, Gary was already in the only bedroom.

"Nobody's here," Gary said over his shoulder. He had the closet door wide open, and Nate could see it was also empty.

"He packed up his stuff and skipped." The disappointment that washed over Nate surprised him. Until that moment, he hadn't known how badly he wanted to break this case.

Gary lowered his weapon and walked toward him. "We might as well call it in and go back to your house."

Nate hated to leave. There must be something they could do, something they had overlooked. Reluctantly he closed the front door behind them and followed Gary to the dock. Gary used his portable radio to report that the man they'd gone to interview wasn't available.

"I guess we can ask Jon and Allison Woods if he brought the boat back and paid for the rental," Nate said. "Or Bridget Kaplin might know if he's left town for good. She handles the cottage rental."

"Sure," said Gary.

Nate hopped down into the boat and waited for Gary to cast off, then started the motor. He pulled out away from shore and revved the engine. Every minute might count, but he couldn't resist the urge to head just a little north by east until he could see Emily's place. Had she gone straight home as she'd promised?

They cruised past the Surpassing Peace camping center and rounded the rocky point until he could see past the other docks to the last one in the row. The first thing he focused on was Emily, standing on the end of the dock and waving a bright red beach towel.

Emily flapped the towel wildly in the breeze. She'd heard the motor before she saw the boat, and hoped it was Nate and that he would look her way. Her heart pounded as she studied the approaching craft. *Nate's boat! Thank You, Lord!* She raised the towel over her head again and waved it in a wide circle. Nate brought the boat in close and turned it sideways ten yards off her dock, causing a deep wave that swept toward the shore.

"What's up?" Nate called. He was in full uniform, including his bulletproof vest, broad-brimmed brown hat, holster, and sunglasses. Gary Taylor, in his blue state police uniform, looked nearly as dashing. Under different circumstances, she'd have teased them about how fine they looked.

Emily gulped and yelled over the pounding waves and idling motor. "Anton Pressey. I saw him leave the island as I was coming home."

Nate nodded. "When?"

"Twenty minutes ago? Maybe a half hour. When I saw you heading for his place, I knew you wouldn't find him."

"Which way did he go?"

She pointed toward Baxter.

Nate and Gary consulted, but she couldn't hear what they said.

"We would have seen him if he went to the marina," Nate called.

"I didn't see where he went, but he started out in that direction." Later she'd tell Nate how she'd jumped back into her own boat hoping to follow Pressey, and in her haste had flooded the outboard motor again.

The two young men conferred for a moment.

"Take me with you," Emily called.

Nate looked at her, his eyes wide, then turned back toward Gary for a moment. She was afraid they would refuse, since they were carrying out official business. But Emily would never live it down if they pulled off the town's biggest arrest of the year and she wasn't there to report on it.

"I'm bringing the boat in," Nate called. Ever so gently, he brought the cabin cruiser closer. When it nudged the wharf's framework, Gary reached out and grabbed the ladder that extended down the side of the dock and into the water. "Jump in quick," Nate said.

Emily scrambled down to the deck, and he immediately pushed the boat away from her dock, urged the engine to life, and swung the boat in a wide circle.

"Where are we heading?" Emily screamed over the deafening whine of the motor.

"The marina."

She nodded and sat down on one of the seats. Gary opened a locker and tossed her an orange life jacket. She buckled it on and sat back. No sense trying to talk until they landed, the motor was so loud. They all scanned the shore, and she concentrated on the boats moored at the marina as they approached, searching for one with a green stripe on the hull. If she'd just been more careful starting that motor again, she could have followed Pressey until she knew exactly where he landed and then intercepted Nate and Gary.

"I think that's his boat." She pointed as they neared the shore, indicating one tied up in a slip and bobbing on the gentle waves. Several of the rentals looked similar, but the green stripe narrowed down the possibilities among the dozens of watercraft.

They docked, and Nate tied the boat. Emily jumped out, quickly followed by Nate and Gary.

"We'd better have a talk with Allison," said Nate. "She might be able to tell us where he went from here."

Allison smiled and waved to them as they entered the marina store. She was finishing up an order for one of the island visitors. "How's it going?" she asked as the customer exited, eyeing the two men in uniform with curiosity.

"Hey, Allison," said Nate. "Did the guy staying in Derbin's cottage turn in his boat just now?"

"Anthony Smithson? He sure did," she said. "He said he was done with the boat and the cottage. He paid his bill and everything, but he seemed in a bit of a hurry."

"Not surprising," said Gary. "I would be, too, if I were him."

"Is something wrong then?" Allison asked.

"It's definitely shaping up that way," said Nate. "Did you happen to see what he did after returning the boat?"

Allison leaned on the counter. "I don't mind telling you as soon as he walked out the door, I followed him and watched to see what he was up to. You asked about him before, and there's a lot of funny things going on around here. I said to myself, just maybe Nate will come around wanting to know about this guy again."

"So, where did he go?" Gary asked.

"He got in his car," said Allison, "and he *wasn't* alone."

"Who was with him?"

"One of the *heirs.* That Jette girl. I'd know her anywhere."

"That must be why we didn't see him on the lake," Nate said. "He went over to the Heron's Nest for Jette. I'll bet he was docked there when we set out for Grand Cat." He turned to Gary. "They're going to hit I-95, no question about it."

"I agree," said Gary.

Emily stepped forward and touched Nate's sleeve. "Jette said she'd stay here in town."

Nate's eyes crinkled. "Yeah, she *said* that."

"They're probably halfway to Canada by now," Gary said.

Nate turned to face him. "You may be right. All the same, we'd better make sure they're not at the Heron's Nest." He said to Allison, "Thanks for your help. I'm glad he at least paid you. Looks like we'd better make tracks."

Emily reached for his hand as they followed Gary out of the store. "Can I go with you?"

Nate hesitated. "We can take you to the Heron's Nest, but if we have to chase those two down, you'll have to stay behind."

"Fair enough," said Emily. "I can go to the office and clue Felicia in, and I'll start writing my story about this for next Tuesday's paper."

"All aboard," Gary called through the window of his cruiser. He had already started the engine.

On the short run to the Heron's Nest, they speculated as to what Anton Pressey was up to, and how he had schemed to kill his ex-wife and get hold of her money.

"I'll bet he started tracking down Stella as

soon as he got out of jail," Nate said. "He's probably been planning revenge for years. Stella testified against him and made sure he got a long, tough sentence."

"So you definitely think he killed Stella?" said Gary.

"Yeah, I do. And then dug up some girl to pretend to be her granddaughter so she could claim the estate and split it with him."

"You still don't think Jette is who she says she is?" asked Emily. "It seems to me that would be a huge risk to take."

Nate shrugged. "Pressey didn't have much to lose."

"I disagree." Emily raised her chin. "He had a lot to lose. Think about it. He's been in prison for *years*. And now he's finally out."

"True," said Gary. "But you'd be surprised how many times these ex-cons blow it a second time as soon as they get out."

"But it's not like he got out last week. He's been free for two years, and if Jette is telling us the truth, he's built a relationship with his granddaughter."

"It could have taken him this long to find Stella," Gary said.

Nate nodded with an apologetic glance at Emily. "I know Jette sounded convincing, but it all could be an act."

"I won't believe that until we have proof." Emily stared ahead, out the windshield, realizing she didn't want either Jette or Jeanette to be proven liars. The idea of either or both girls going to prison tied her stomach in knots. "Jette probably doesn't know he killed Stella. She thinks she's just helping her nice old, misunderstood grandpa."

They arrived at the bed-and-breakfast, and Nate and Emily got out.

Rita was relaxing in the sitting room with a paperback novel when they entered. "Hi, Nate. Hi, Emily." She pushed herself up off the sofa.

"Hi, Rita," Nate said. "I need to know if Jette Williams is still here."

"She checked out about an hour ago." Rita's smile drooped. "Is something wrong?"

"Maybe. Was anyone with her when she left?"

"No, I don't think so. She carried all her luggage downstairs herself."

Nate sighed. "I hope we aren't too far behind them."

"What's going on?" Rita asked.

"I'll explain," said Emily. She turned to Nate. "You go ahead. Be careful."

"I will." Nate gave her hand a squeeze and turned toward the door just as Gary mounted the porch steps and opened the front door.

"Call it in," Nate said as he walked toward his cousin. "Jette's on the loose. Checked out an hour ago — right before Allison saw her and Pressey together."

Gary's eyebrows shot up. He glanced at Emily, gave her and Rita a nod, and followed Nate toward the car.

"I think Nate's wrong," Emily said to Felicia a few minutes later in the *Journal* office. "I don't like to disagree with him, but this doesn't make sense to me."

"What?" Felicia poured coffee for both of them.

"Anton running away now, if he went to all that trouble to find Stella and kill her. He didn't cut and run as soon as she died. He wanted Stella's life savings. So why take off now?"

"Good question. He knew the police had ID'd him yesterday, and he didn't run then. So what do you think he's up to, Miss Super Sleuth?" Felicia asked.

Emily sat in her swivel chair and curled her hands around her mug. "I think he must have been very angry and determined if he planned to kill her. He had forty years to let his bitterness against her simmer. And forty years to plan this thing in great detail. And he wanted her estate, so he got Jette up here to help him. Why is he giving up now?"

"He must think the police are close to pinning Stella's murder on him. Did you get enough out of Nate and Trooper Taylor to start writing a story?"

"I think so. Anton's apparently skipped town, so Nate said it's okay to reveal his identity."

But as Emily started a new computer file, she found she couldn't concentrate on the few facts she knew. She pondered Anton's possible intentions, and what he would do if he knew he was suspected but didn't have the estate yet.

"You know," Felicia said, "forty years is an awfully long time to serve for armed robbery."

Emily nodded. "A man was shot in that escapade. And Nate got me some more information on Pressey's police record. He got out of jail once, but he got caught for stealing again within a matter of weeks and got put right back in the slammer. And then he was released again and was arrested on a parole violation. The time he served wasn't all for that original charge."

Felicia sipped her coffee and set her mug down. "He probably blames Stella, anyway.

Some men do that — blame anyone but themselves for the mess they've made." She resumed her typing.

"Felicia?"

"Huh?" Felicia looked at Emily but kept typing.

"Can I pop out for a minute or two? I have a hunch."

Felicia laughed. She tucked a strand of hair behind her ear. "Go ahead, but I want to hear about this hunch when you get back! Does it have to do with Stella's death?"

"Everything to do with it." Emily jumped up from her desk. "I should be back soon." She hurried out of the office and to Nate's yard, where she kept her car during her stays on the island. If her hunch was right, there was no time to lose.

She drove out of town and headed for Stella's house. Sure enough, as she pulled up on the side of the road, she spied a car parked in the driveway.

She felt certain it was Anton Pressey's vehicle, and that he was inside the house poking around. She whipped out her cell phone.

"Nate? Hi, it's me. I'm parked outside Stella's house, and there's a car here."

"What are you doing there?"

"I don't know. I had this feeling something

wasn't right." She rolled down her window as she talked and squinted at the unfamiliar car.

"Em, you've got to be more careful. Get out of there, and Gary and I will come back and check it out."

"Can you run the plate number for me first?"

"Sure, give it to me."

Emily smiled at the resignation in his voice. She read off the number and then waited for his response.

"That's Anton Pressey's car."

"Thought so." Emily stared toward the house, but it looked as quiet and peaceful as ever. However, the yellow crime scene tape hung limp on the porch instead of stretching across the closed front door.

"Has anyone seen you?" Nate asked.

"I don't think so. The police tape is down."

"Get out of there now, Em. We'll be there in thirty minutes. Go back to the *Journal*."

Emily closed her phone and put the car in reverse. Just as she was about to turn around, she heard a shrill scream from the direction of the house. Instinctively, she put the transmission in park again and jumped out. She couldn't let one of the girls get hurt. It would take Nate and Gary half an hour to get there. Maybe the simple act of making her presence known would stop something bad from happening.

She dashed across the lawn and up the steps of the porch, took in a deep breath, and knocked on the door. *Nate is going to kill me,* she thought.

A moment later the door was opened by Anton Pressey. He stared at her for a moment then lifted a gun and pointed it at her face.

16

Anton grabbed Emily's arm and yanked her into the house. His grip brought tears to her eyes as he walked her toward the kitchen, the gun pressed against her jaw. He shoved her through the doorway.

Emily knew better than to struggle against someone holding a gun. She stumbled into the room, sensing other people on the far side of the dim kitchen. Anton pushed her toward the wall near the table, and she stood meekly, looking down at the floor where she'd found Stella's body just over two weeks ago. She had foolishly placed herself in the killer's power. *Lord, keep me safe,* she prayed. How near was Nate? He'd said half an hour.

"Now we got trouble," Anton said gruffly. "This nosy newspaper reporter wants a big story. Well, she's gonna get a story. Tie her up, Jette."

Jette? Emily looked up. Her eyes adjusted

to the dimness. Jette stood across the room, wearing the same black jeans, striped T-shirt, and zippered sweatshirt Emily had seen her in earlier, watching her from beneath furrowed brows. Not far from her, tied to one of Stella's gray-painted Windsor chairs, sat Jeanette. Her dark eyes contrasted with her pale face. Jeanette pressed her lips tightly together and met Emily's gaze. Rope bound her ankles, below the hems of her plaid capris, securing her feet to the chair.

Emily swung her gaze back to Jette and made eye contact for a second. She tried to convey her confusion without words, but Jette quickly looked away.

"Sit down!" Anton pulled a chair out from the table.

Emily walked over hesitantly and sat. Jette began to tie her up, pulling the knots snug, but not so tight that the strands bit into her skin. Emily fought back the urge to blurt out her feelings of betrayal. She had known all along, though she hadn't wanted to believe it, that one of the two girls must have been lying about her identity and her purpose for visiting Baxter. But still, she had wanted to trust Jette. The girl seemed to need someone to trust her.

"Now, where were we? Oh, yes. My money." Anton trained his gun on Jeanette.

"The attic? The basement? Where is it?"

Jeanette blinked hard and tears filled her eyes. "I don't know! I told you a million times. I don't know anything about any money."

Anton stepped closer to her chair. "Is it buried in Mason jars in the backyard? Stella never did trust banks."

Jeanette choked and said nothing. A tear ran down her cheek.

He came closer and bent over, leaning his elbows on the kitchen table and holding the gun almost casually. "Don't make me use this. I'll find that money with or without your cooperation."

"She's not budging," said Jette. "Either she's determined to hold out on you, or she really doesn't know."

"Never mind," said Anton. "We'll keep looking. Stella would have stashed it somewhere real clever, same as me. That's how she got ahold of it in the first place. She stole it all off me while I was in jail."

The contempt in his voice made Emily shiver. She couldn't imagine being married to someone like that. Stella must have lived in terror during her marriage to this man.

"It took me a long time to find her, you hear me? When she got out of jail, she took that money — my money! She snatched it and dropped out of sight. She thought I'd never find her. But I did, and I'm not leaving until I get that money back."

"I don't know where else to look," said Jette.

Anton absently pointed the gun toward the ceiling and scrunched his eyes up until they were small, glittering orbs. "You're looking in the wrong kinds of places. She wasn't stupid. No tissue box or mattress stashes for her. She'd put it someplace where that no-good husband of hers wouldn't find it. He probably never knew about the stash she stole from me. I'll bet he thought she was innocent and honest." He let out a bitter bark of a laugh.

Jette leaned with her back against the refrigerator. "You look then. I'm tired of searching."

"You're tired," he spat out. "Some help you turned out to be. I didn't do you a good turn to be backstabbed like this. You were supposed to establish yourself as the old woman's heir, move in, and find the money on your own. But, oh, no. You couldn't manage it by yourself."

"They wouldn't let me move in," Jette retorted. "The *police* wouldn't let me!"

"I knew you were a fake," said Jeanette.

"Shut up!" Anton hollered at her. Jeanette

cringed and lowered her chin to her chest. "Come on," he said to Jette. "That's a dirt floor down in the cellar. She probably buried some of it down there when she first moved in."

"Did it occur to you that she might have spent the money to buy this house?" Jette's upper lip curled, causing her lip ring to glitter as it caught the rays from the light over the sink.

"This dump? Not all of it, trust me. Thirty years ago this heap wasn't worth much." He yanked open the door to the cellar way.

"Hadn't I better stay up here and watch them?" Jette asked.

"If you've tied them tight enough, they won't go anywhere. Do I need to check those knots?"

"No, they're good," Jette said, flicking a glance at Emily.

Emily held her breath. Was Jette telling her to try to escape when they left the room? She pulled against the ropes and turned her wrists as far as she could, but her bonds felt secure.

"That news story said there was cash," Anton said.

Emily cleared her throat. "Actually, what I wrote was that the attorney indicated the estate was worth more than just this house.

That doesn't necessarily mean cash. It could be stocks, mutual funds, life insurance . . ."

"Oh, you're so smart." His narrowed eyes shot daggers at her. Rusty, jagged daggers honed in prison. "I oughta make you dig."

At least she wouldn't be tied to a chair then. But did she want to dig a hole while Anton Pressey held a gun on her? Shudders ran down her spine. That hole might become her grave.

"We looked that floor over really well," Jette protested. "It's all hard-packed dirt that hasn't been disturbed. It would take weeks to dig it all up, and you'd find zilch."

Anton hesitated at the top of the stairs and looked back at her. "If she buried it years ago, before she married that Lessard guy . . ."

"Why would she do that?" Jette asked. "She'd want it where she could get at it and use it if she needed money."

"The flower beds," he said with a decisive nod. "She could dig them up every year, and no one would be the wiser."

"Hey, that's a thought," Jette said. "Soft ground. But that Cedar guy might have found it." She swung around and looked at Emily. "Didn't he do a lot of the gardening?"

"I . . . think it was more after Mr. Lessard

died," Emily said. "I know Cedar cut firewood for Stella, but he did seem to be doing yard work, too, these past few years."

"Like mowing the lawn?" Jette asked.

Emily shrugged. "One thing you can be sure of is that Cedar doesn't have much money. If he'd found a hidden treasure, the whole town would know about it. He's not one to hide his emotions."

Anton closed the cellar door. "I think we should dig up the flower beds. We've gone over this house from top to bottom. Unless there's a secret compartment we didn't find, it ain't in here."

Emily imagined Anton scooping up shovelfuls of Stella's daffodils and lilies, throwing them willy-nilly about the lawn. It might keep him busy until Nate and Gary got here.

"Did you see a shovel?" Anton asked Jette.

"Don't think so."

He turned on Emily. "You knew her. Where would she keep a shovel? There wasn't one on the porch or in the basement."

"I don't know." Emily saw his eyes darken and his jaw clench and added hastily, "But there's a shed in the yard. There may be some tools out there."

"There *is* a shed," Jette said. "I searched it yesterday." She peered out the window that faced the woods on the side of the house away from the road. Emily figured she could see the tool shed from there. "Hey, Gramps! Someone's out there."

Anton strode to the window. "Where?"

"I saw a light, like maybe a flashlight. It went around toward the front of the house."

Emily's heart hammered. Were Nate and Gary here so soon? They wouldn't know Pressey was armed. They would see her car in the driveway, though.

"Come with me." Anton hurried toward the entry, and Jette followed him out of the kitchen.

Emily exhaled. "Are you all right, Jeanette? Did he hurt you?"

Jeanette sniffed. "Not much. He shoved me around and slapped me once. I think he figures I knew Stella before she died, but I didn't." She blinked her damp eyelashes and whispered, "Honestly, Emily, I never met her. And if she had some money to hide, I have no idea where she would have put it. This is the first time I've ever been inside this house."

Emily nodded. "The man is desperate. Over the years, he's built this up in his mind. I mean, how much could it have been? A few thousand? A million?"

"I doubt it was that much," Jeanette whispered.

"Me, too. But he's rationalized it all in his mind. Stella testified against him and because of that, he spent more time in jail than he would have otherwise. She got a light sentence as part of the deal. He figures she retrieved his loot when she got out, and came here and hid. She started a cozy new life. Now he wants his money and his life back. But he won't find it here."

"Are you sure?" Jeanette sniffed.

"Yeah, pretty sure. Stella wasn't stupid. She had a safe. If there was cash, I presume she kept it in there, along with her important documents. But the safe is no longer here."

Jeanette stared at her, then glanced toward the doorway. The murmur of low voices came from one of the front rooms.

"You mean, there was a safe in this house when she died? Those two didn't find one, that's for sure."

"Yeah, there's a reason for that. You know Nate, my fiancé?"

Jeanette nodded.

Emily whispered, "He and another officer removed the safe the day Stella died, to hold it secure for her heir. They took it to the Penobscot County Sheriff's office. I think it's locked up there, unless they had it put in a bank vault or something. It's not here anymore."

Jeanette swallowed hard and looked toward the doorway again. "Are you going to tell him?"

Emily shrugged, but that made the ropes pull against her wrists. "If it will save our lives, sure. Why not? Maybe he'd let us go if he knew that."

Doubt clouded the girl's eyes. "I don't know. He probably wouldn't believe you. And if he did, it might make him madder than he is now, if he knew it was someplace where he couldn't get at it. What if he . . ." Jeanette shivered.

"Jeanette, I've been praying hard and trying to think of ways to distract Anton. See, I called Nate before I came in here. He and another officer should be here soon. It could be one of them that Jette saw out the window. Or maybe she imagined something. But if it's not them, maybe we could convince Anton to start digging up your grandmother's flower beds. That would keep him and Jette busy until —"

A gunshot shook the house.

17

Emily's ears rang with the repercussion. She wished she could get her hands up to her ears. Jeanette grimaced as though in pain and squeezed her eyes tightly shut.

"Are you all right?" Emily could barely hear her own words. Jeanette must not have heard her question. Slowly the roaring in her ears faded, but a ringing remained. A bitter taste filled her mouth. What had Anton done?

Movement drew her gaze to the doorway, where Anton entered, followed by Jette. Anton's mouth moved as he walked, but the only words Emily could make out were ". . . crazy old guy."

She caught her breath. "Did you shoot Cedar?" Her voice sounded faraway, beyond the ringing.

Anton threw her a glance and laughed.

Jette came over to her chair and leaned toward Emily. "He didn't. He just scared him away."

Emily inhaled deeply, wondering if anyone in the neighborhood had heard the gunshot. Stella's home nestled in a secluded wooded area. The closest house was Cedar's, and that must be half a mile down the road.

Jette's dark eyes roved about the room, not resting long on anyone. Was she frightened by Anton's show of force? Emily closed her eyes and tried to calculate the time that had passed since she'd called Nate. If Cedar wasn't hurt, would he go to Nate when the police car drove up? And could she use what time she had left to turn Jette against her grandfather?

She opened her eyes. Anton was rummaging through the kitchen cabinets. They must have searched them already. He took down a can of ground coffee and set it on the counter.

"Jette," Emily whispered. The girl ignored her. *Her ears are probably ringing worse than mine.* Anton laid his pistol on the counter and struggled with Stella's coffeemaker. Louder, Emily said, "Jette."

The girl snapped her gaze to Emily's face and raised her eyebrows.

"You don't have to help him," Emily said softly. "You can get out of this now. But if you stay in it with him, you'll face criminal charges, just like your grandmother did."

Jette's lip curled. "I knew you were smart, but now you've got a law degree."

Anton glared over his shoulder. "Shut up. Jette, come make me some coffee. Does this thing need a filter?"

Jette pursed her lips and gave Emily a dismissive look before joining him. "I'll get it, Grandpa."

"Great. I knew you were good for something."

He didn't see the hurt look on Jette's face as he turned away, scooping up the pistol, but Emily saw it. *Lord, help me to get through to Jette. Open her eyes and let her see how wrong it is to help him.*

"Okay, Peaches and Cream." He walked over and stood squarely in front of Jeanette, giving Emily a profile view of his sardonic features. "Stella must have told you something. Spill it."

"I told you, I never met her." Jeanette's voice trembled.

"I don't believe you."

"Too bad." Jeanette's face reddened and she cringed. Anton swung his left arm and slapped her.

"What are you doing?" Emily pulled against the ropes but only succeeded in making the chair wobble. "Leave her alone!"

Anton rounded on her, shoving the gun toward her. "Shut up!"

"She's your granddaughter." Emily glared up at him. "Don't you realize, she's as much your flesh and blood as Jette is?"

"That's it." Anton whirled away and stalked to the counter. "Gag that one," he said to Jette. "I can't stand her lip anymore."

Jette pushed the button to start the coffeemaker and looked over at Emily. She hesitated, looking about the kitchen. "What do you want me to use?"

"Anything. Just shut her up." Anton prowled out into the hallway again.

Jette gulped and opened several drawers. She pulled a few dish towels and washcloths out, looked them over, and chose one. Straightening, she approached Emily slowly. "I have to do this. I'm sorry. I know you don't mean any harm. If you promise not to yell at him, I'll make it loose."

Emily nodded, eyeing the threadbare towel she'd chosen. "I'll be quiet, for your sake and Jeanette's. That man is capable of extreme violence, Jette. I don't want him to hurt you or Jeanette any worse than he already has."

"He's never laid a finger on me." Jette's mouth was a thin purple line as she rolled the towel the long way to improvise a gag.

"He will, sooner or later."

Jette's eyes flashed. "Grandpa's right. You talk too much."

As she tied the towel around Emily's face, Emily looked over at Jeanette. The girl was slumped in her chair, sobbing quietly. Jette knotted the ends of the towel behind Emily's head, but not too tightly. Emily pushed against the cloth with her tongue. At least it was clean. She prayed that someone had heard the shot and called the police, but even so, Nate and Gary were no doubt the closest officers. A call would warn them that Anton was armed, if nothing else.

Anton walked back into the kitchen. "Seems quiet out there. Now, let's get down to business." He stood before Jeanette again and reached to raise her chin. Jeanette lifted her eyelids, staring up at him with watery eyes. Her mouth twitched.

"Last chance, Peaches. You must have found out where she kept her dough. That's why you were so mad when you found out Jette beat you to it and got to town before you did."

"No. That's not true." Jeanette's tears flowed freely, and she jerked her chin away, lowering her head against her shoulder.

"Listen to me." Anton waved the pistol across her line of vision. "You give it to me straight, or I'll shoot the reporter girl. You get me?"

Bile rose in Emily's throat. Was this the end?

Jeanette straightened her shoulders. "Okay, I'll tell you where it is. She had it in a safe."

Anton froze and stared at her. Emily's chest hurt. Would the revelation that the police had put Stella's assets out of his reach anger him to the point of killing her and Jeanette? She tried to cry out, but only a small groan echoed in her throat.

"A safe?" Anton and Jette moved closer to Jeanette.

"There's no safe in this house," Jette said.

"That's right. The police took it."

All was silent for a moment. Jette looked up at her grandfather. "If the police have the money, there's no reason to stay here, Grandpa. We'd better leave."

"No. No, I won't do that until I either have the money or know there's no hope of getting it."

"That lawyer is probably holding the money for the estate." Jette plucked at his sleeve. "Come on, Grandpa. Let's go."

Anton shook her hand off. "No. She wouldn't stash it all in one place. There's got to be some hidden here." He looked around wildly. "Stella was always like that — every time I brought home some loot, she'd hide it."

His gaze lit on Emily. She sensed evil as he stepped around beside her and watched Jeanette. A heavy dread settled over her. He raised the muzzle of the pistol to Emily's temple and glared at Jeanette.

"Are you telling me the truth, Peaches? I meant it when I said 'last chance.' "

Emily's head spun, and she found it hard to breathe.

"Yes!" Jeanette's eyes widened and she strained at her ropes. "Don't shoot her. The police *did* take the safe. But it's —" She choked on a sob and lowered her gaze.

"It's where?" Anton's steely voice cut the air.

Emily tried to still the thumping of her heart. *Please, Lord, if You want me to die, at least let Jeanette know You're real and that You care about her. Help Jette to see this man is evil.* A fleeting thought of Nate racing toward the house to help her sent tears gushing into her eyes. She blinked and stared across at Jeanette, feeling the hard end of the gun's barrel against her temple.

Jeanette glared up at Pressey. "It's out on that island."

Emily felt Anton flinch. The gun moved

slightly, and she held her breath.

"What island? Grand Cat?"

Jeanette nodded. "The police put it out there because they figured you'd never look for it there. It's in Emily's cottage."

Nate called the dispatcher and reported the plan for him and Gary to drive to Stella Lessard's cottage near Blue Heron Lake and sat back, his stomach doing flips. If they arrived before Anton Pressey left the house, they would be confronting a hardened ex-convict. He wasn't looking forward to renewing the acquaintance.

"Should we put the siren and lights on?" Gary asked.

"Let's not. There's not much traffic tonight, and we don't want to give him advance warning that we're on the way."

"Right." Gary accelerated as they came onto a straight stretch leading toward Aswontee. "So you think he's in there looking for valuables?"

"I don't know what he's doing, but I doubt he's picking up souvenirs." Nate gritted his teeth. Why had he been so sure that Pressey would try to flee the state? He and Gary had put a good twenty-five miles between them and Baxter before Emily's call came in. Now they had to retrace their steps. At least Emily was safe. She should be over at the *Journal* office with Felicia by now, sipping chai tea. He was thankful for that.

"I guess I'll give Emily a call and make sure she's someplace far away from there." He took out his cell phone and punched in her number.

"What's the matter?" Gary asked a moment later.

"She didn't answer. I got her voicemail."

"She probably left her phone in her car."

"Yeah." Nate started to return his phone to his pocket but decided to try the newspaper office instead.

"*Baxter Journal.* This is Felicia Chadwick."

Her matter-of-fact voice calmed him, and he relaxed his clenched fingers a bit. "Hi, Felicia. This is Nate. Is Emily with you?"

"Actually, no. She left here . . . oh, maybe forty-five minutes ago. Said she had a hunch about Stella's death."

Nate's stomach tied itself in double knots. "And she hasn't called in?"

"No. What's up, Nate?"

He made himself exhale slowly. "She called me twenty minutes ago from outside Stella's. Said Anton Pressey's car was parked in the driveway. I told her to amscray and go back to the office. But I tried to call her just now, and she's not answering her phone."

"She . . . hasn't come back. Should I go over there?" Felicia asked.

"No. Gary and I are on the way. We'll get there in about ten more minutes. You couldn't get there much faster."

"Okay. I'll stay here and call you if she comes in."

Nate clicked his phone shut and reached for the switch that would activate the light bar on top of the car. Why couldn't Emily keep out of trouble? But then she wouldn't be Emily. He glanced over at Gary. "Floor it."

"Untie them," Anton growled, indicating Jeanette and Emily with a wave of his pistol.

Jette stepped forward and bent to work on the ropes that held Jeanette to her chair. When her hands were free, Jeanette brought them to her lap and rubbed her wrists.

"That sounds fishy." Anton eyed Jeanette for a long moment. "Why would they take it all the way out to the island? I mean, putting a safe in a boat . . ." His face brightened and he swung around to look at Emily. "You and your boyfriend might do something like that. If you knew there was cash in it, you might have seen a good opportunity to get yourselves a little nest egg." He nodded as though he liked the idea. "You came here that day. You and that nutcase gardener."

Emily's heart thudded in her chest as she speculated on what his ramblings meant. Was Anton here the day she came to interview Stella? Had her arrival — or Cedar's, before her — scared him away before he found the safe?

Jette glanced up at Anton. "Say, maybe we should leave them tied up while we go and check it out, Grandpa. It wouldn't take long."

"Leave them here alone? No. That old guy might come back and help them get away and call the cops."

Jette's purple lips pouted as she fumbled for the rope around Jeanette's ankles. "It just doesn't make a lot of sense to me that anyone would haul a heavy safe out to the island. Does that sound logical to you?"

Anton hesitated. "How about if you stay here with these two? I'll go back to the marina and get the boat again and run out there."

Jette let out a short laugh and stood. Jeanette bent to pull the loose rope away from her legs.

"You couldn't lift that safe by yourself," Jette said, smiling at him with a shake of her head. "What would you do if you found it?"

Anton frowned and stepped over next to Jeanette. "You wouldn't lie to your old grandpa, now would you, girl?"

Jeanette caught her breath. "No, sir." She stared down at the floor.

He swung around and leveled the gun at Emily. "Take the gag off her, Jette."

As the girl worked at the knot behind her, Emily waited, her heart and her mind racing. Jette pulled the cloth away, and she licked her lips, trying to get rid of the dry, cottony taste.

"All right, you get one chance," Anton said, pronouncing each word distinctly. "Is there a safe?"

Emily nodded. "It took three men to get it out of here the day Stella died."

Anton swore and paced to the refrigerator and back.

"What can we do?" Jette asked. "Could you open it if we found it?"

"Maybe. Can't blow it open, that's for sure. Someone would hear the explosion. And that's if we had any explosives, which we don't." Anton paced the kitchen again. He stopped near the cellar door and whirled to face Jette. "We'll shoot them both so they can't tell where we went. Then we'll go to the island."

"No!" Jette jumped forward, holding both hands out toward him. "You're kidding, right, Grandpa? We couldn't do that."

Anton eyed her for a long moment, then shrugged with a chuckle. "Right. I was just trying to scare them."

Jette exhaled. "Good. Because if we get caught, we're in enough trouble as it is. I don't want anything to do with . . . with hurting people."

"Trouble?" He fixed Jette with a glare that sent shivers down Emily's spine. "You don't have a clue about trouble, girl. If these two are lying to me, they'll be sorry, I'll tell you that. Stella stabbed me in the back. Well, she got hers in the end, didn't she? It took me a long time, but I made sure she got what was coming to her."

Jette stared at him, her dark eyes like hollows in her pale face.

"Don't look so shocked, kid. You knew we were here for the money. When the newspaper came out with the story that said her estate had some value beyond this sorry old house, I knew she'd been sitting on my loot all this time. I'd suspected as much before, but she denied it. Well, who's going to end up with it now? I'll tell you who. You and me, that's who."

Jette moved slowly over to Emily's chair. "I . . . I'll untie you now. Don't try anything."

"You'd better not." Anton's voice rose. Emily was sure that Cedar or anyone else outside could hear him plainly. "I deserve that money, and I'm going to get it. I've worked hard, and I'm not leaving until I get every cent. Things didn't go right at first, so I went to all the trouble of playing tourist and getting Jette up here to put in a claim as an heir." He gestured toward Jeanette with the gun. "Come on. Stand up. You girls may come in handy."

Emily swallowed hard. She couldn't let him take her and Jeanette out of the house. How would Nate and Gary find them?

"So, are you and Jette going to go off and live together once you get your — your money?" She nearly choked on the words, but she managed to hold his gaze steadily.

"I dunno," he muttered. "I figured to leave Jette here to live on the property, but if the cops find out she was helping me, they won't let her inherit. And I don't have any guarantees that you and Peaches, here, will keep your mouths shut."

"I won't tell anyone," Jeanette said quickly. "I'll go home and not ask for a share of the estate. Just let me and Emily go. I promise,

I won't turn you in."

"Oh, sure," Anton said with a sugary smile.

"I won't. Honest."

"Shut up!"

Jeanette jumped back, tipping over her chair.

Emily wanted to rail at him, but this wasn't the time to go after a bully. Instead she drew a deep breath and squared her shoulders. "Mr. Pressey, I won't tell, either. Let us go. I'll even tell you exactly where the safe is."

"Oh, you'll tell me, all right. Because you're going with me. You'll show me. But first we need a boat."

Emily opened her mouth, then clamped it shut and stooped to right the fallen chair. Not the time to tell him the police had the safe in a secure place, not on Grand Cat. That might be just enough to stimulate his trigger finger again.

18

"You two take my car," Anton said, tossing Jette his keys. "Make Peaches and Cream drive. I'll take the nosy reporter with me. No sense letting anyone find her car here." He shoved Emily toward her car. She stumbled and caught herself against the door panel. Where was Nate?

Over his shoulder, Anton called to Jette, "Make her drive you straight to the marina. Stay right behind us. No tricks." He took Emily's keys from her and unlocked the passenger door. "Get in."

She climbed in and reached to close the door, but he held it open.

"Oh, no, sweetheart. Slide over. You're driving."

Her stomach lurched. He'd made her get in on his side to keep her from locking him out and to allow him to keep an eye on her while he got into the car. Once he was settled, he reached for his seatbelt and buckled it. So she couldn't hope to stage a minor accident and throw him against the dashboard. With trembling hands, she buckled her own belt.

He handed her the key ring. "All right, back out nice and easy. Don't try anything cute. I don't need you, and I'd as soon put a bullet in you and dump you out in the ditch, you understand?"

She couldn't speak, so she nodded.

"Good. Let's go. Baxter Marina. You know the way, I'm sure."

She made herself breathe slowly and evenly. Darkness had fallen, and she put the headlights on as she backed carefully onto the road. Behind them, Jeanette pulled out a few seconds later in Anton's car. She wouldn't dare try to escape, even though Jette was unarmed. Would she? Emily thought not. Anton had terrorized her thoroughly. Jeanette would do as she was told.

Sending up a fractured prayer, Emily glanced at Anton. He held the gun below the level of the windows, but it was pointed at her midsection.

"You should leave Jette out of this," she said.

"Ha! Right." He shook his head. "She wants the loot as much as I do. She's got nobody now, except for me. I promised her she could keep the house. I get the cash, and she gets the real estate. She doesn't want to cut and run now."

"Are you so sure they'll declare her the rightful heir to Stella's estate?"

"Why shouldn't they?" he snarled. "She's Stella's granddaughter, all right. If that other clueless girl hadn't shown up and ruined everything, the estate would have been settled by now, and I'd be out of here."

"Are you saying Jette is your granddaughter, but Jeanette is not?"

He frowned and seemed to consider the question seriously. Emily braked at a stop sign and looked hopefully both ways on the main road but saw no sign of the police car. What would she do if the squad car appeared on the road, coming toward her? Flash her lights? Slam on the brakes? Hit the horn? And how would Anton react if she did any of those things?

"At first I thought that Jeanette was an impostor," he said. "Jette never said anything about a sister. But then I got to thinking she might be playing it straight. And if she is really Lois's girl, then she might know something. I was right. She told me where the money is."

Emily said nothing but eased out onto the

main road and guided her car into the marina store parking lot. Only a few cars sat in the lot. Nate's SUV sat over to one side, near his house, where he usually parked it. The lights were on in the store, but Nate's house was dark. Jeanette brought Anton's car in behind them and parked, slightly crooked, in the space next to them. Jette got out on the passenger side and walked around to talk to Anton.

He lowered his window. "All right, kid. You take the snoopy one inside and get us a boat. I don't want anyone to see me here again."

Jette stooped and looked in past him, catching Emily's eye for just a moment. "Okay. What will you do, wait out here?"

"I'll swap cars and take your wannabe sister down the shore a ways. You two rent a boat and come pick us up."

"Where?" Through the window, Jette passed him the keys to the other car. "Over at the Heron's Nest, where I was staying?"

"Nah, they'd see you and recognize you. Isn't there a public boat landing thataway?" He pointed in the opposite direction, away from most of the town's businesses, and looked expectantly at Emily.

"Yes, there is." She felt like a traitor, even giving him that much.

"Pick us up there," Anton said. "There won't be many folks there this time of day." He turned and bored into Emily with his dark gaze. "You behave yourself, hotshot. Jette won't have a gun on you, but I'll still have Peaches and Cream. If the two of you don't show up at the landing in fifteen minutes with a motorboat, or if the cops show up, she's a goner. *Capice?*"

A huge lump formed in Emily's throat. He would do it. No doubt about that. She nodded.

"All right, then, get going."

He got out of the car and stuffed the gun in the pocket of his light jacket. In the moment when he was halfway out and she was opening her door, Emily picked up her purse. If he told her to leave it behind, she'd tell him Allison and Jon might want a deposit on the boat.

By the time Emily took the few steps to join Jette, Anton was already in the other car with Jeanette. She took a deep breath, glad to be free of his presence for a short time. As she'd expected, Jeanette had stayed put and not tried to bolt. She must be terrified, alone with Anton in such a tight space. Emily looked back and saw the girl cringing against the driver's door as he settled in beside her.

"Come on," Jette said. "We've got to pick them up, get out to your place, and get that money before the police are onto us."

Emily inhaled deeply and squared her shoulders. Now all she had to do was give a Tony-winning performance. Keep Anton calm and stable, that was the mission of the moment. She shot a silent prayer heavenward.

They stepped through the door into the marina store.

Jonathan poked his head out from one of the food aisles. "Hello, ladies," he said. "I'm just about to close up. How can I help you?"

"Act casual," Jette hissed in Emily's ear.

"I know." Emily tried to keep her voice steady. "We need a boat. Nate and Gary brought me to the shore earlier today, so my boat's still out on the island."

Jonathan walked to the counter carrying a box of cereal and a half gallon of milk. "All right, no problem. Let me cash myself out first so I don't forget. The last thing I want to do when I get home is turn around and come back here for Cheerios and milk." He grinned.

Emily tried to laugh but it came out sounding more like a cough or a suppressed sneeze.

"You going to spend the night on the

island?" Jonathan asked, choosing a set of boat keys from behind the counter.

Jette's chin jerked up. "Uh, yeah," she mumbled. "I'm staying with Emily."

Emily tried desperately to think of a way to give Jonathan some kind of hint about what was going on. If she could catch his eye, maybe she could let him know she was scared. He'd probably only ask her if she was okay. There was no time to give a clue.

"Well, have a good evening." He handed the keys to Emily. "Boat seven is a little bigger than yours, but you can handle it. It's a very reliable motor. You don't need to pay for that. Just bring it back in the morning."

"Thanks." Emily smiled grimly. There had to be a way to tip him off without alerting Jette, but she seemed to have brain freeze.

In the near twilight, the two girls walked down to the water's edge and found the boat. Emily climbed in and started for the driver's seat.

"Oh, no," said Jette. "This time I'm driving. Gimme the keys."

Emily shrugged her shoulders and handed Jette the key ring. Maybe she could call Nate while Jette focused on getting the boat to the landing where Anton and Jeanette waited.

"Cast off, and sit right there." Jette

pointed to the seat beside the driver's. "I don't want you trying anything when I'm driving."

Emily went to the bow to untie the painter that held the boat in place. If she were going to call Nate it would have to be now. She fumbled with the rope, pretending she couldn't get it loose. Carefully, she slid her cell phone from her pocket with her left hand.

"Hurry up!" Jette called.

Emily flipped her phone open and called Nate on speed dial.

Gary pulled the cruiser into the driveway of Stella's house. The yard was empty. No cars, and no sign of life.

"Emily's cleared out, anyway," said Gary. "That's good."

Nate nodded slowly. *But she's not with Felicia. Where is she?*

Gary got out of the car. "Looks deserted to me," he said. "But we'd better scope it out in case someone's still in there. You armed?"

"Yeah." Nate got out and peered at the dark house.

"I figure if anyone was in there we'd have seen some curtains moving when we drove in," Gary said. "You go ahead and I'll cover you."

"Right." Nate drew his gun and advanced toward the house. "Hello!" he called. "Anyone in there?"

There was no answer, except for crickets chirping in the tall grass behind the house.

"This is the police," Nate called again. "We're coming in."

He stood to the side of the front door and tried the knob. The door swung open, and his pulse quickened. This was not good, not good at all. Where *was* Emily? If Anton had seen her car . . . Quickly he checked the thought. He had to keep his mind on the task at hand.

He stepped into the entry, leading with his pistol. All was silent. Gary followed behind him into the dimness of Stella's living room. "Are there lights in here?"

"I think the electricity's still on," said Nate. He flipped the wall switch near the door, and light flooded the room.

"Hey, anybody in here?" Frustration laced Gary's voice. They both hated chasing a dead end. But surely somewhere there was a clue to what was going on. Emily had definitely seen Anton's car parked in the yard; he wouldn't have come poking around here for no reason.

"Pressey!" Nate advanced toward the kitchen and turned on the lights there. The smell of fresh coffee filled the air. "Jette? Jeanette?"

"There's no one here," said Gary.

"Wait up," said Nate. He squinted into the shadows of the kitchen. Were those ropes on the floor?

"What?" Gary stepped up behind him.

Nate walked over to the kitchen table and crouched next to one of the chairs. "Look at this."

Gary whistled softly. "That doesn't look good."

Nate stood again, glancing around the room. He spied the coffeepot, a red light indicating it was keeping the fresh brew warm. "Care for a cup of coffee?" He reached over and turned the machine off.

Gary leaned against the doorjamb. "This is weird."

"Whoever was here left in a hurry," said Nate.

"Something must have scared him off."

Cedar? Or Emily? Nate prayed that Anton hadn't seen Emily. There was no telling what he'd do to her if he thought she knew what he'd done to Stella. He felt a surge of anger welling up inside him. If that guy hurt her . . .

His cell phone rang. He yanked it out of his pocket and looked at the screen. Emily! "Em, where are you?" He waited, but there was no answer. Suddenly a sputtering roar reached him. A motor starting. He'd bank on it being a boat motor, probably a medium-sized Johnson. "Hello? Em, what's going on? Are you okay?" All he could hear was the drone of the motor. After a few more seconds, the line went dead.

"What is it?" Gary asked.

"Emily called, but she didn't say anything. And I heard a boat engine starting and running. But she can't get reception on the island."

"She must still be on the mainland, somewhere in Baxter," Gary said.

"Or headed out to the island in a boat."

"Maybe she was calling to tell you she was going home, but the connection was no good on the lake," Gary suggested.

"We have to find her." Nate headed back through the house toward the front door.

As he bounded down the steps, leaving Gary to turn the lock on the door, a dark figure burst from behind a lilac bush beside the path. Nate pulled up, reaching for his pistol.

"Nate!" a deep voice called.

His heart settled back into his chest, and

he let go of the pistol's butt. "Cedar! You scared the daylights out of me. I told you to stay away from here."

"I know you're mad." Cedar ducked his head but stepped forward, his hands outstretched. "She shot at me this time, Nate."

"Who shot at you?"

"That girl. The metal-mouth girl. Her or the man."

Gary joined him and eyed Cedar sternly. "What's going on here, Cedar?"

"Jette Williams," Nate said. "She and Pressey shot at him."

Cedar nodded eagerly. "First they went inside with another lady. They weren't supposed to, but he made the door open, and they went in. Then Emily came and they shot at me."

"Whoa, whoa, whoa," Gary said.

"No, don't stop," Nate said. "Tell us where they are. Where's Emily now?"

"I don't know. I thought they were going to kill me, so I ran. But after awhile I came back, and the cars were leaving."

"Emily's car?"

Cedar nodded, his breath coming in shallow gasps. "Hers and that man's."

"And Jette had a gun?"

"I didn't see the gun when they went in." Cedar threw a troubled glance toward the house. "But somebody shot at me out the parlor window. That was after Emily went in. And then they all left. But I don't know where they went."

Gary looked at Nate. "What you heard on the phone — that motor."

Nate nodded and clapped Cedar on the shoulder. "Thanks. I'll talk to you again later."

He and Gary rushed to the police car.

"Where to?" Gary asked.

"The marina."

"That's what I was thinking. And time to call for backup."

Nate placed the call then flipped on the strobe light. As they cruised into town, he tried to organize his thoughts enough to pray, but all he could think about was Emily in the power of Anton Pressey. *Please help her,* he managed. *God, please help her.*

Gary turned in at the marina's parking lot. Nate spotted Emily's car at one side. There was still a light on in the store. "Wait here," he said. "I'm going to see if she's inside."

Gary stopped the car in front of the door and Nate hopped out.

"Keep your eyes peeled." Nate mounted the steps, just as Jonathan opened the door.

"Nate, I was just locking up when I saw

your lights. Can I do something for you?"

"Yeah. Have you seen Emily in the last couple of hours?"

"Emily? Sure, I have. She just left." Jonathan smiled, then glanced past him at the police car. "Is everything okay?"

"How long ago was she here?"

"Oh, maybe ten or fifteen minutes ago. She and that punk-looking girl came in to rent a boat."

"Jette?"

"Yes, that's the one. I'd have been out of here by now, but right after they left in the boat, Marvin and Rocky Vigue stopped in wanting a part for Rocky's old Evinrude, so I'm slow getting out of here tonight."

Nate frowned. Ordinarily, he'd be glad to know Rocky and his father were doing something together, but his brain straight-lined to Emily. "Did you see that man, Smithson? The one who was renting the Derbin cottage?"

"Not tonight. I thought he'd left town."

"And did Emily say where she was going?"

"She and Jette were going to spend the night at her cottage. Nate, is something wrong?"

"Ask me tomorrow." Nate ran down the steps and opened the door of the cruiser. "Come on, Gary. My boat. Hurry."

Emily grasped the edge of her dock and pulled the boat in. Anton held the gun on her while she tied the boat and climbed out. He growled at Jeanette to get out as well.

"Is that your cottage?"

"Yes." Emily looked back across the dark water, toward the marina. Was Nate at Stella's house now? The lights of the little town taunted her. She had let a criminal take her away from help. She should have told Jon Woods to call the cops. At least she'd be safe now if she had. But a glance at Jeanette, who shook from head to foot as she stood on the dock, skewed things back to reality. No way could she leave Jeanette alone in Pressey's clutches to save herself.

"Okay, let's get up there and get at that safe." Anton climbed precariously from the boat, and Emily hoped for one fleeting moment that he was going to fall into the lake.

She wasn't close enough to topple him and his gun into the water, but while he recovered his balance, she surreptitiously untied the boat again and dropped the loop of rope onto the seat.

"All right, ladies, let's move." He nodded in the direction of the cottage but held the gun down at his side, away from the lights of the Vigues' cottage next door.

Emily headed up the path. The others' footsteps sounded behind her. She mounted the steps to the porch and opened the door. They all trooped across the screened porch and inside the cottage, clustering about her in the kitchen as they looked around.

"All right, reporter girl, where's the safe?" Anton said.

Emily saw Jeanette glance at her nervously. She wanted to lie to Pressey, to tell him it was buried in the backyard, or it was upstairs, anything to confuse him for a few more minutes and give her a chance to escape. But she knew it was useless to bluff any longer. She took a deep breath. "It's not here."

She watched the anger boiling up inside him, his eyes flaming. He cursed. For a moment he seemed too consumed with emotion to form any coherent thoughts. She hoped he wouldn't strike out at her or Jeanette. She glanced at Jette and saw concern on her face, too, as she watched her grandfather. At last he drew in a deep breath. "So, where is it?"

"The sheriff's men took it," said Emily. "It's locked up someplace safe, to keep it secure for Stella's heir."

He lifted the gun and pointed it at her face. Her pulse raced and her stomach heaved.

God, help me!

A hammering sounded on the door.

Anton swore and swung toward it, leveling the gun at the window in the porch door. Emily's muslin curtain kept them from seeing who had knocked.

"Hey, Emily, are you okay?"

She closed her eyes for a moment, feeling lightheaded. Rocky Vigue. Not Nate, not Gary. She'd even be glad to hear Detective Blakeney's voice right now. But Rocky?

"I saw a boat drifting near your dock, so I brought it in and tied it up for you," Rocky called through the door. "It looks like one of the marina boats. Emily? Are you in there?"

Anton pulled the trigger and sent a bullet crashing through the door.

19

Emily slapped her hands to her ears and went to her knees. Her ears rang and her heart thudded wildly. As the shock of the blast receded, she became aware of Anton, still standing with the gun held out before him, glaring at the door, and Jette and Jeanette both huddled under her kitchen table.

Lord keep us safe!

She rubbed her ears and swallowed. Acrid smoke hung in the air, and she heard yipping — distant barking, like that of a small dog shut in a closet.

Clinker, of course. Rocky never went anywhere without his dog. Was Clinker's master lying on her porch bleeding with the little mongrel standing guard over him? *Help Rocky, Lord! If he's hit, please don't let him die.*

Anton turned and looked down at her. "Get up."

Emily stood, but her legs felt like limp string. Jette crawled from beneath the table, not taking her eyes off her grandfather. Jeanette remained where she was, and even from several feet away, Emily could see that tears bathed her face and she was shaking.

God, this is my fault. I should have told him the safe wasn't here the minute he took my gag off. Show me what to do now!

"How many windows in the next room?" Anton barked.

"Uh, two." Emily could barely hear her own words.

"Get in there."

She forced her legs to move.

"You!"

She jerked around at Anton's shout. He stooped and peered under the table at Jeanette, who had scooted back as far as she could against the kitchen wall.

"Get out here. Now!"

Clinker still barked, his annoying, monotonous cries demanding attention. A hole splintered the panel of the front door, just below the bottom edge of the curtains. Emily swallowed hard as Jeanette crept out on all fours. Just for a second, Emily caught Jette's gaze. The girl trembled, and she shrank back, watching Anton with wide, unblinking eyes.

■ ■ ■ ■

Nate eased his boat in gently, turning it sideways to Emily's dock. One of the marina boats was tied on the other side. As soon as he'd looped the painter around the ladder railing, Gary was over the side and clambering up onto the dock. Nate followed.

As they ran toward the cottage, he heard a dog barking nearby. A large figure loomed out of the shadows beneath the pines and came toward them.

"Hey! Over here! That you, Nate?"

"Rocky?"

"Yeah. I think I'm shot."

Nate grabbed his friend's sleeve and pulled him off the path and into the inky shadow of the big trees. Clinker stopped barking and galloped toward them, careening down the path. "What happened? Do you need a doctor?"

"I don't think so, but I'm not sure. My arm is bleeding. The guy shot right through the door."

"Is Emily in there?"

"Yeah."

Nate caught his breath. He wanted to be angry at her, but his fear chased away the "you-should-have-listened-to-me" thoughts.

"Tell us what happened, if you can. Do you need to sit down?"

"I think I'm okay," Rocky said. "My dad and I came over from the marina. After we landed, I took Clinker for a walk. I saw a light on at Emily's so I figured she'd come home for the night. I looked down toward the dock, and I saw her boat tied up, and another boat floating a few yards out. That was weird, so Clinker and I went out on the dock to take a closer look. The boat was going to drift away. So we got in Emily's boat and went to tow the other one back in and tie it up. Didn't we, fella?" He stooped to pat Clinker's head.

"Did you say you were shot?" Gary asked.

"Well . . ." Rocky straightened. "When I went up to the cottage to tell Emily about the boat, she didn't come to the door. I could see a little bit between the curtains. There was kind of a crack, see. Just a little one."

"Yeah, yeah! Cut to the chase." Rocky's hurt look made Nate feel slightly guilty, but every second might matter for Emily and the Williams girls.

"I saw Emily," Rocky said. "And Jeanette and that other girl, the one with the spiked hair. And a guy with a gun."

"What did this guy look like?" Gary asked.

"I dunno. I just saw the gun in his hand and then I realized he was pointing it toward the door. So I jumped to the side just as he pulled the trigger. I wasn't thinking about how he looked."

"Are you sure you got hit?" Nate asked. "You don't seem to be hurt bad."

"My arm hurts. Look." Rocky pulled his elbow around with his other hand and craned his neck to look at his upper arm. "Maybe it grazed me. Or maybe it was a piece of the door."

Gary pulled his flashlight from his belt and focused the beam on Rocky's arm.

"It's not bad. You'll be fine."

"Hey, Rocky! What's going on?" a voice called.

"Oh, that's my dad." Rocky looked toward the Vigues' cottage. "He must have heard the shot."

"Go tell him everything's under control, but you all need to stay over there," Nate said.

"If it's under control, why —"

"Just go. And take Clinker."

"Get someone to look at that wound," Gary added.

Rocky eyed them for a long moment. "Okay, Nate. Whatever you say."

"Thanks, Rocky. I'll come over to see you

later." Nate watched his friend waddle away and turned to Gary.

"What do you think?" Gary asked. "It could be an hour or two before backup arrives."

"Yeah. I think we should try to establish that all the girls are alive and well."

"Right. You want to talk to Pressey, and I'll see if I can sneak around the perimeter and get a look inside?"

"I don't have a better plan." Nate sucked in a deep breath. "Lately I seem to be thanking God often for Kevlar."

"I know what you mean." Gary patted the front of his protective vest. "Don't leave home without it. Especially when you're dealing with a gun-toting, crazy ex-con." He melted into the shadows.

Nate walked cautiously up the path, keeping to the side and watching the porch and front windows. He saw no flicker of movement, but the kitchen light glowed. He decided to use the steps on the left side of the screened porch, instead of the ones that led directly to the front door. Tiptoeing to keep his footsteps silent, he worked his way up the three stair treads and sneaked along the porch, hugging the house wall until he reached the high window over the kitchen sink. He stood on tiptoe and peered in from the extreme edge of the window frame. From that angle, he couldn't see anyone. He bent low, passed under the window, and worked his way to the door. Sure enough, the wood panel below the small window was splintered.

Ever so slowly, he leaned over and put his face near the glass, making use of the gap between the short curtains as Rocky had. The kitchen appeared to be empty.

"Pressey!"

Emily jumped and cocked her head toward the kitchen. She would know Nate's voice anywhere. *Thank You, Lord!*

"Pull those blinds," Anton growled.

She glanced at him, and he moved the pistol slightly and nodded toward the living room window. The rustic room was Emily's favorite at the cottage. Anton now leaned against one of the two old armchairs facing the large fieldstone fireplace, where she and Nate had lounged many an evening. Jeanette cringed in a ball on the sofa, and Jette seemed to be checking out the bookcases that completed the furnishings. The open stairway rose at one side, giving access to the two bedrooms and bath above, but so far no one had ventured upstairs.

Turning toward the casement to obey Anton, Emily caught a slight movement outside. Someone was on the ground below the window. She stood still for a moment, focusing. Gary Taylor moved his head out away from the wall outside, so she could see him better. He lifted two fingers to his right temple in salute, then placed them over his lips.

Instead of nodding in reply, Emily managed a quick smile, trusting that Anton wouldn't catch her expression in the reflection from the glass. She pulled the blind's cord, shutting Gary from her view. So he and Nate were both on the island, and they knew her situation. She hoped they'd been able to help Rocky.

"Anton Pressey, come out here," Nate shouted.

"That's Nate Holman, Emily's boyfriend," Jette told her grandfather. "He's a cop." Emily's heart lurched.

Anton turned toward the kitchen and yelled, "No chance, Holman! I like my odds better in here."

"Let the girls go, Pressey."

Anton walked into the kitchen. Emily heard the scrape of a chair across the bare floor. He returned a moment later with a grim smile fixed on his face.

"Do you hear me, Pressey?"

"I hear you. Shut up or I'll start shooting."

"Pressey, listen to me. I need for you to let the girls go. Send them out here to me. Then we'll talk about whatever it is you want."

"I don't want nothing from you, Holman. Go away."

"I'm not leaving."

Anton grimaced and gestured with his pistol for Jette to move closer to the fireplace. "Sit down, kiddo. Put that stonework between you and the overzealous cop."

"He's worried about Emily," Jette said, staring at her grandfather. "They're getting married, you know."

"So I've been told." Anton swore and turned on Emily, who still hovered near the window. "That's how they found out who I was. You came with those stupid cookies. How could I have fallen for that lame trick?"

She cleared her throat. There was nothing she could say to appease him.

"Pressey!"

"Shut up, Holman, or I'll put a bullet in your cute fiancée's skull."

Emily grabbed the edge of the bookcase to steady herself. Jeanette pulled her legs up, wrapped her arms around her knees, and hid her face in her arms.

"Let's be reasonable," Nate said. "You're only digging yourself in deeper. You may as well give up."

Anton walked to the kitchen doorway and lounged against the jamb as he listened to him.

"We've got a bunch of cops out here. Put your weapon on the floor and come out."

"Not going to happen."

"Then let the girls go," Nate called.

"No way."

After a short silence, Nate's voice came again. "Pressey, let me at least see the girls. Show me that they're all okay."

"Why wouldn't they be okay?"

"You just threatened to kill one of them."

"Ha!" Anton spun around and grabbed Jeanette by the arm, jerking her up from the couch. He held the gun at her spine and pushed her ahead of him into the kitchen. "Can you see this one, Holman? She's the fake. I'm not claiming her as mine. Is she alive enough for you?"

With Anton out of the room, Emily looked at Jette. She had half risen from her armchair but settled back down now, listening.

"What is it that you're after, Pressey?"

After a long moment, Anton spoke again. "Three things. I want my money, Holman.

That and a boat to take me to the mainland."

"That's two," Nate said. "What else?"

"Clearance to the Canadian border."

Nate looked at Gary. Both stood on the porch now, between the front door and a window. Gary arched his eyebrows.

"What do you think?" Nate whispered.

His cousin shrugged. "Keep him talking if you can. The girls all look healthy. One of them looks scared out of her gourd, though. Can't blame her. Just keep stalling him until we can get some backup and a negotiator."

Nate leaned toward the door without exposing himself beyond its thin panels and window. No sense standing in the most likely path of a bullet.

"I'll have to talk to somebody higher up about that and see what they say," he called to Pressey. He turned back to Gary and whispered, "You can use your radio, right?"

"Should be able to."

Nate nodded. "Go down to the dock. He won't hear you, and you might get better reception there. Find out what the status is on our backup. And hurry. I don't have any experience with this kind of situation."

Gary tiptoed to the side of the porch, where steps went down to the path to the woodshed. Nate watched him go cautiously in the other direction, toward the shore. Rocky's bulky form emerged from the trees, and Gary halted beside him.

"Hey, what's going on?" Rocky's voice carried clearly to Nate on the porch.

"Hi," Gary said. "You need to go back to your place."

"Mr. Kimmel heard the shot and came over to ask us what happened," Rocky said.

Gary glanced up at Nate, and Nate lifted his palms in an exaggerated shrug.

"Okay, here's what you need to do." Gary placed one hand on Rocky's shoulder. "We need your help here, to make sure everybody is safe. Tell your folks and your neighbors and anyone else who's out here on the island — even Raven Miller and the staff at the conference center — that they need to stay put and not come over here, okay?"

"Sure. Me and my dad can do that." Rocky squared his shoulders.

"Good. Because we've got a sticky situation here. More police are on the way, but it will take them a while to get out here. We need all the civilians to keep their distance and not interfere. We don't want anyone in the way. Someone could get hurt."

"Don't I know it. My mom put a bandage on my cut."

"Not too deep, I hope?"

"Nah, she says it's only a scratch. Musta been a wood sliver."

Gary nodded. "Okay. So far everybody's fine inside Emily's cottage, and we're trying to make sure it stays that way. You understand how important this is, Rocky. Make sure all the people know to stay away."

"Has that guy with the gun kidnapped those girls?"

"I can't tell you any more right now. I need to get on with my job. You do yours, too."

"I will." Rocky turned and shuffled toward the Vigue cottage, and Gary headed toward Emily's dock.

"Jette!"

Jette swung her head around in response to Emily's urgent whisper.

"You should surrender to the police. I can tell you how to get outside without Anton seeing you."

"Why would I do that?"

Emily huffed out a sigh. "Don't you get it? If you don't give yourself up, you'll spend the next few years at least in jail."

"I don't think so. Grandpa's got things under control."

"Oh, right." Emily shook her head. "He's

not getting out of this, Jette. Look, so far nobody's been badly hurt." She tried not to think about Rocky. Best not to mention him right now. "You might be able to plea bargain for a light sentence at this point, especially if you testify against Anton."

"What, stab him in the back like Grandma did?" Jette rolled her eyes. "What do you think I am? He needs someone he can trust, for once in his life."

From the kitchen, Anton's voice came, harsh and defiant. "Yeah, well, forget about talking anymore."

A tear trickled down Jette's cheek. She wiped it on the sleeve of her sweatshirt. "I don't want to go against him."

"Think, Jette!" Emily glanced toward the kitchen. "Remember what he said at Stella's house? He made sure she got what was coming to her. You know what that means."

Jette blinked rapidly and a small sob escaped her lips.

"What do you think will happen to you?" Emily leaned forward. "Do you think he'll set up a home with you in Canada? He didn't mention your name when he asked for safety to the border. And even if he does take you along, you'll never make it that far. You'll never even make it to the marina. I'm telling you, Jette, your only chance is to give up. I've been praying for you all week —"

"Shut up!" Jette jumped from her chair and stood staring into the empty fireplace.

In the kitchen, Anton shouted angrily, "Just come back when you have an answer for me. I'm walking out of here, Holman. Nothing else is acceptable."

His heavy steps plodded toward them, and Emily sat back. Jette straightened her spine and turned as Anton pushed Jeanette into the room.

"Sit down again, Peaches. You're not going anywhere until that cop gets me what I want." He looked rapidly from Jette to Emily and back again. "What's going on in here?"

"Nothing." Jette sniffed.

Anton's mouth slid into a snarl. "Don't you talk to them, you hear me?" He swung the gun toward Emily. "I'm getting sick of you. If you talk to my granddaughter again, you've had it."

He marched back to the kitchen and screamed, "Holman! You out there?"

Nate's muffled voice replied, "Yeah, Pressey. What do you want?"

"Your girlfriend is just about finished. If she messes with my grandkid again, I'll use her for target practice. Now, hurry up and set things up the way I told you!"

20

"You got anything to eat in this dump?"

Anton's restless prowling about the room had kept Emily on edge for ten minutes. Both Jette and Jeanette had avoided her gaze, but now Anton's question focused everyone's attention on her.

"Yes. Sure. Uh, I have sandwich makings and . . ." She thought of the steak in the freezer she'd been saving to share with Nate some evening. Maybe she wouldn't mention that. "There are some hot dogs in the fridge and a little leftover potato salad and chicken stir fry." She racked her memory for the groceries she had on hand. "Oh, and cereal. Apples. Crackers."

"Make me a sandwich." He walked toward her, holding the gun at waist level.

"Sure." Emily stood slowly. Her mother's training took over. "Would you girls like something?"

Jeanette looked up at her with bloodshot

eyes and shook her head.

"I'll take a hot dog," Jette said. "Got any buns?"

"Yes, I think so. Maybe you could help me." Emily looked to Anton for approval.

"Sure." His sardonic smile did little to calm her butterflies. "You two go have a chum-fest in the kitchen. And if the cops try to talk to you, nothing doing. You keep your mouth shut, hear?" He glowered at Emily until she nodded. "Go." He dropped into the chair Jette had vacated.

Emily scooted into the kitchen, out of range of his malevolent glare. One of her kitchen chairs was tipped, with the back wedged under the doorknob. If she tried to move it and unlock the door, Jette would yell for her grandfather.

"What are you waiting for?" Jette asked.

Emily opened the refrigerator and pulled out mustard and a package of sliced salami.

"Could you put these on the counter, please?" She handed the items to Jette. "Let's see, you wanted a hot dog."

Jette deposited her items on the counter and leaned against it, folding her arms across her stomach. Emily hoped she could use Anton's momentary calm to influence the girl. If he bounced back to the violent mood, her chance would be over. She smiled at Jette. "Not the way I planned to spend the evening, but . . ."

"I suppose this fouls up all your notions about God and how He'll make sure nothing bad happens to you."

Emily arched her eyebrows. "Not at all. God never promised that bad things wouldn't happen to His children. But I know He's here with me, and no matter what happens, He'll take care of me. Even if that means your grandfather kills me tonight."

They stood still for a moment, watching each other. Jette looked away first.

"Hey, do you have any relish? I like relish on my hot dogs."

"Here you go." Emily handed her the jar. "The buns should be over there in the breadbox."

She put a hot dog apiece for herself and Jette in the toaster oven, then added a third. Jeanette might change her mind when she smelled them cooking. While they broiled, she got out paper plates and spread mustard on whole wheat bread for Anton's sandwich. A moment later Jeanette came into the kitchen with him close behind.

"Sit down," Anton told her, and Jeanette pulled out a chair and sat at the table, never raising her eyes.

"Whatcha got to drink, Miz Gray?" He edged over to one of the windows and pushed the edge of the curtain aside a fraction of an inch with the barrel of his pistol then peered outside for a moment.

"Uh, milk, grape juice, diet cola, and water."

He laughed. "Lake water?"

"Poland Spring water. I buy it by the case."

"Gimme the grape juice, if you haven't got anything stronger."

"That's it," Emily said, striving for a casual tone.

"What, that strapping big cop of yours doesn't want a beer now and then?"

"Nope. He's a milk drinker."

Jette chuckled. "I knew he was a Boy Scout the minute I met him. That's probably why he's so tall." She opened the toaster oven. "You got a potholder, news girl?"

"Here." Emily grabbed one off a hook by the stove and tossed it to her.

Jette caught it and grinned. "Thanks."

Emily opened the salami package. Why couldn't they just be friends? None of this craziness, just she and another girl, talking about guys and food and God. She turned and smiled at Jeanette across the room, but she was staring down at her hands, folded on the pine table.

"Jeanette, can we fix you a hot dog or a sandwich?"

"No, thank you." Her voice cracked.

Was she close to breaking down? Emily walked across the room, ignoring Anton's stony expression. She slipped her arm around Jeanette's shoulders.

"It's going to be okay. This will be over soon."

"Yeah," Anton said. "As soon as they get us a boat and a ticket to Canada." He turned and looked toward the window. "I hear an engine. Do you hear that?"

They were silent for a moment, and Emily caught the sound of an outboard motor.

"I hear it, Grandpa," Jette said.

"All right!" Anton leaned over to peek out the edge of the window again. "I see lights on the water. Looks like a couple of boats."

"Are they coming in to the dock?" Jette asked.

"No, it looks like they're going to tie up next door."

"That's our neighbors', the Vigues', dock," Emily said. "It could be them getting home late."

"Nah. It's cops. Hey, Holman!"

His sudden shout startled Emily. Jeanette

cringed and turned her head into Emily's side. Emily stroked her hair and whispered, "It's okay."

No one answered Anton's shout. He swore and looked over his shoulder at them. "Where's my sandwich?"

Emily let go of Jeanette and moved back to the counter. "Coming right up." She quickly finished making the sandwich and cut it in half. She picked up the plate and held it out to Jette.

Jette just looked at her.

Emily raised her eyebrows and nodded toward Anton. With a scowl, Jette took the plate and walked over to the window.

"Here, Grandpa."

Emily poured a glass of grape juice and set it on the table. Anton pulled out a chair, but before he could sit down, Nate's voice came from outside the house.

"Pressey! Do you hear me?"

Anton walked toward the door and stood sideways between it and the window. "I hear you. Are you ready to deal?"

"We're working on it."

"You'd better be."

Jette watched him with huge brown eyes. "Grandpa," she whispered. "Don't let them stall too long. They'll get a whole bunch of cops out there, and then they won't let us go."

"Hey, Holman!"

"Yeah?"

"You got thirty minutes to arrange things."

"That's not long enough."

"That's all you get."

"Listen to me, Pressey," Nate called. "We can't even use a phone out here. In order to call the Border Patrol, we had to send someone in to shore. We're relaying what you want, and we have a lot of people working on it, but we're not ready yet."

Anton rubbed the back of his neck. "It's not that complicated."

"Just be patient, Pressey," Nate said. "My boss would hustle things along quicker if you could just let one of the girls go."

"Forget it! You got thirty minutes. If you're not ready to let us go then, the nosy reporter is dead."

Footsteps retreated down the porch steps. Anton stuck his pistol in the back of his waistband and picked up the glass of grape juice. He took a sip then slammed the glass down on the tabletop.

"What's wrong with you people, not having any beer?"

"The neighbors might have some," Jette suggested.

Anton's eyes flickered.

"I could ask," Emily said quickly. "Marvin Vigue might have some. I could go over and ask and come right back with it."

Anton barked a laugh. "Oh, sure, you could." He glared at Jette. "Make me some coffee. I didn't get to drink it the last time."

"Sure." Jette's eyes pleaded with Emily. What could she read there? "Help me humor him"? "Show me where the coffee is"? Or . . . "Get us out of this mess"?

Emily stepped to the counter and pulled the carafe from the coffeemaker. "Grab a couple of those water bottles from the carton over there, will you, Jette?"

Anton stomped into the living room, carrying the plate with his sandwich. Jeanette let out a wrenching sob as soon as he left the room. Emily set down the carafe and went to wrap her arms around the weeping girl again.

"I never should have come here," Jeanette gasped.

Emily leaned over and tugged a paper napkin from the holder on the table and held it out to her. Jeanette snatched it and pressed it to her eyelids.

Emily patted her shoulders. "It's going to be okay."

Jeanette sniffed and glanced up at her.

"Do you still think God will get us out of this alive?"

"Yes, I do."

"Are you praying now?"

"Every minute. Do you want me to pray out loud?"

Jeanette shrugged. "He might get mad."

Emily knew she meant Pressey. She glanced toward the next room. Anton paced back and forth, from the fireplace to the stairway. She bowed her head close to Jeanette's and whispered, "Father, preserve us. Calm us and show us Your strength."

She opened her eyes. Jette scowled at her from across the room.

"Grandpa wants his coffee."

Emily gave Jeanette a quick squeeze and released her. "I'll get it. But it's decaf."

Jette gritted her teeth. "Don't tell him. And make it strong."

Once more, Emily eyed the chair wedged beneath the doorknob. How many seconds to pull it out, throw the bolt, and run out the door? How many more seconds before she heard a gunshot behind her?

She started the coffeemaker then looked over into Jette's sullen face. "God will forgive you if you ask Him to," she whispered. "We'll help you all we can. Not just Nate and me. The police will help you, too.

Please don't do this, Jette. You know what's right."

Another boat puttered up to the Vigues' dock and the engine stopped. Two officers climbed out onto the wharf.

"All I've done is talk to him a little and try to make sure the girls aren't in distress," Nate told the senior state police officer, Detective MacRae, who had arrived fifteen minutes earlier.

Gary hurried up from the dock, to where Nate and MacRae stood near the Vigues' grill. "It's the negotiator."

"Great," MacRae said. "You did a good job, Holman. You, too, Taylor."

Nate pressed the light button on his watch. "He said we only had thirty minutes about twenty minutes ago." He was surprised when a female officer joined their huddle.

"Trooper Anderson, this is Deputy Holman," MacRae said. "Anderson's the negotiator we've been waiting for."

Nate shook her hand. "I'm glad you're here. We only have a few minutes left before the suspect's ultimatum expires."

"And then he starts shooting hostages?" Anderson asked.

"Yeah." Nate swallowed hard.

"You think he'll do it?"

Nate glanced at Gary, who nodded. "I do," Nate said. "He's already shot at two people tonight. He missed one, and the other was only superficially wounded, but yeah, I think he'll follow through, and this time he'd be so close he could hardly be expected to miss."

"All right, I'm going up and talk to him. I understand we can't get phone service out here, so I guess it has to be in person."

"That's right," Nate said.

She eyed the cottage. "They have electricity, though."

"It's a generator. I thought of disabling it to make Pressey less comfortable," Nate admitted, "but I wasn't sure that was a good idea. But I could do it for you now if you want."

She shook her head. "It would put them in the dark, which could be more dangerous for the hostages. Unless this situation lasts until daybreak, I'd say let's leave that generator alone." Anderson gestured to the officer who had arrived with her. "Let's go, Bob."

"There's one other thing," McRae said.

Anderson stopped and looked up at him. In the light that spilled from the Vigues' cottage, Nate saw her arched eyebrows and taut features.

"Holman's fiancée is inside."

Trooper Anderson looked at Nate for a long moment. "Maybe you shouldn't be here."

"He was first on the scene," MacRae said. "We can't ask him to leave now."

She nodded. "All right, but stay out of it now, Holman. We'll get her out."

The lump in Nate's throat grew until he could barely breathe past it as he watched the other officers deploy into the shadows around Emily's cottage.

Anton prowled around the kitchen and living room while the coffee brewed. Jeanette edged her chair as far out of his path as she could and shrank against the wall. Jette devoured her own hot dog and the extra one, washed down with a can of diet cola. Emily realized she was hungry and ate hers, too.

"Jette —" She broke off as Anton entered the kitchen again. Every time she tried to resume their earlier conversation, he reappeared and swore at her.

He paced to the window that gave the best view of the waterfront.

"Looks like they've got reinforcements." He leaned heavily against the woodwork, peeking out and muttering.

"The coffee's done." Emily went to the counter and poured a mug. "What does he take in it?" she asked Jette, not wanting to ask Anton directly. He accepted communication through Jette more cordially.

"Black." Jette took the mug Emily held out to her and gave her a long stare before she turned toward her grandfather. What was going on behind those wildly made-up eyes?

Jette walked softly across the kitchen and stood a pace behind Anton. He didn't turn around but continued his vigil, watching from behind the curtain.

Instead of speaking to him, Jette stepped forward and snatched the pistol from the back of his waistband, jumping back and sloshing an ounce of coffee onto the linoleum. Emily caught her breath.

Anton whirled with a snarl and lunged for Jette. Before he could speak, she jerked her arm, throwing the scalding coffee in his face.

By the time his scream hit her ears, Emily had a sharp knife in her hand. Jeanette still cringed against the far wall, but Jette faced Anton, holding the pistol before her with shaking hands.

"Don't move, Grandpa."

"You little —" He pounced, barreling

toward her with his arms raised.

The gun roared just before he slammed into Jette. The impact sent them both careening into the table and shoved it toward Jeanette, pinning her against the wall.

Emily dashed for the door and yanked the wedged chair free. She dropped the knife, threw the bolt, and pulled the door open.

21

A gunshot shattered the night. Nate caught his breath and looked at Gary for a second. They both ran for Emily's cottage. Anderson, MacRae, and half a dozen other officers beat them to it, converging on the front porch. The door opened and light spilled out onto the porch, with a slight figure silhouetted in the door frame.

"Help!"

"Emily!" Nate pounded up the path. By the time he'd reached the porch steps, Anderson had pulled Emily to one side of the door.

"Are you all right?" the officer asked.

"Yes, but —"

"Em, I'm here." Nate folded her in his arms.

She sobbed and threw her arms around him. "I'm okay. Really."

"Get her away," Anderson said.

He pulled Emily along the porch to the

side steps. When they reached the ground, he led her into the shadows beneath the pines. Several officers entered the cottage, and a lot of yelling followed. A trooper dashed out the door and down the path toward Vigues' wharf.

Emily trembled, and Nate pulled her close against his side and kissed her hair. "You scared me good this time, Em. What happened in there?"

"Jette. She got the gun from Pressey."

"We thought she was helping him."

"She was. Until the last." Emily swung around and hugged him, and he held her, watching the porch. "I talked to her every chance I had, trying to convince her that he would only get her deeper into trouble."

"So, was anyone shot?" Nate almost didn't want to hear the answer, but she straightened and looked at him, her eyes wide.

"Anton. I think. He ran right at Jette, and she pulled the trigger. At least, that's how it seemed to me. I think the gun went off before he hit her, but then everything was crazy, and I got the door open and . . ." She buried her face in the front of his Kevlar vest. "I'm so glad you're here."

He stroked her back. "Me, too."

"Should you be helping them?"

"No. They told me to keep clear."

"Because of me?"

"Yes. But there's no place I'd rather be right now than here with you."

She squeezed him, and he stooped to kiss her. August 15 couldn't come soon enough.

Noise at the front door drew his attention. He and Emily watched with their arms around each other as Trooper Anderson led Jeanette onto the porch.

"Are you sure you're not hurt?" Anderson asked.

"I don't think so." Jeanette rubbed her abdomen. "I want my mom and dad."

Emily looked up at Nate. "I should go to her."

"Come on."

They walked to the front of the cottage and met Jeanette and Anderson as they came out the screen door and down the steps.

"Jeanette, I'm sorry this happened to you." Emily spread her arms, and Jeanette dove into them, sobbing.

Anderson eyed Nate in the semi-darkness. "Everything okay with you and the future Mrs.?"

"Yes, thanks. Can we help you now?"

She nodded. "Take Miss Williams over to the dock next door. Maybe get her a blanket or a jacket. She seems a little shocky. The trooper at the boat can radio shore. Her parents need to be notified."

"Should we ask Nicholas Williams and his wife to come to Baxter?"

"Wouldn't be a bad idea, if they're able." Anderson turned to Jeanette and Emily. "Miss Williams, Deputy Holman is going to try to get word to your parents that you're safe. We wouldn't want them hearing about this on the news and worrying about you."

"Thank you." Jeanette clung to Emily, shaking all over.

The look of consternation on Emily's face told Nate that the word *news* had triggered an avalanche in her brain. He would bet she had the story all planned but was frustrated because she couldn't write it now.

Emily pulled in a deep breath and smiled at Jeanette. "Let's go over there with Nate. Maybe we can get a boat to the mainland and you can call your parents when we get there."

Nate glanced back toward the porch. Gary and another officer led Jette out in handcuffs. The girl's short, dark hair stuck up from her head like a porcupine's quills, and her mouth was a dark slash in her pale face.

"Watch your step," Gary said. He hopped down and held out a hand to steady Jette as she maneuvered the stairs.

Nate leaned close to Emily's ear. "Just a sec. I want to touch base with Gary."

"We'll head for Vigues' dock," Emily said. "Come on, Jeanette."

Nate waited for his cousin to reach the path. "How's everything inside?"

Gary grimaced. "Emily's going to have to repaint her kitchen. Pressey's in bad shape, but they're taking care of him." With a glance at Jette, he added, "Tell you all about it later."

"Okay, thanks. If I leave before you do, stop by my house before you head home."

Nate hurried over to Marvin Vigue's dock. Marvin and Rocky hovered, trying to get chummy with the trooper who stood by the high-powered radio in the largest boat at the dock. *They must have gotten Jonathan to open the marina,* Nate noted. At least five of the rental boats were now tied up at Marvin's wharf, and more boats buzzed toward them across the water from Baxter. Nearer the Vigue cottage, a cluster of people waited. Truly and the Kimmel family for sure, and he thought he saw Raven and a couple of her staffers. Nate hopped down into his boat and pulled a blanket from one of the lockers.

The two young women approached slowly, with Emily guiding Jeanette over tree roots and onto the dock. Nate went to meet them and wrapped the blanket around Jeanette's shoulders. By the time they reached the boats, the trooper had gotten through to the local police in Jeanette's hometown.

"Miss Williams, if you'll let Deputy Holman take you to the mainland, you should be able to call your parents from there," the officer said.

"Do you want to go over to the marina?" Nate asked Jeanette.

Her face was a stark white. "I want to go home."

"Maybe we should just take you straight to the lodge." Nate looked doubtfully at Emily.

"She should be checked over by a doctor, I think, Nate."

Jeanette shuddered, and Nate had the distinct impression that only Emily's support kept her from crumpling to the ground.

"I want my mom," Jeanette wailed.

Emily's sorrowful gaze wrenched Nate's heart. No need to ask which mother Jeanette wanted.

"There's an ambulance waiting at the marina," the officer told him. "The EMTs can look her over and decide whether she needs to go to a hospital."

"Do your folks have a cell phone?" Nate

301

asked Jeanette.

Jeanette nodded.

Nate turned to the trooper. "If you have contact with her parents, tell them to come to my house beside the marina. We'll call them as soon as we get to shore."

Nate got mugs out of his cupboard the next afternoon and lined them up on the counter for Emily to fill with coffee. Saturday had dawned gray and cold, and a drizzle had started around noon. All of his guests had accepted his offer of coffee.

"Ward will want milk and sugar." He walked to the refrigerator, took out a gallon plastic jug, and sniffed the contents. "Good."

Emily chuckled. "Some would say you need a wife."

"Yeah? I've got that assignment covered." He bent to kiss her cheek.

"Do you have a cream pitcher?" she asked.

"Uh, yeah, somewhere. I guess." He opened another cupboard. *Where did Mom keep it all those years? Or did she take it to the parsonage when she moved?* He spotted it next to the butter dish he never used and set it on the counter.

"Go ahead in." Emily placed the mugs on a tray. "I'll get this."

"Thanks."

Detective Blakeney, Ward Delaney, and Gary Taylor were making themselves at home in Nate's living room. With no police station in Baxter, Nate had suggested the marina house as a convenient location to debrief on Saturday afternoon.

He nodded at Blakeney. "Coffee's coming right up."

"Good. This won't take long. Just want to bring you all up to speed, since you played such a major role in the situation last night."

"Not me," Ward said sheepishly. "Thanks for letting me in on this."

"Well, you were there at the start of it," Blakeney conceded, "and you're Holman's partner. I have to say, he handled himself well last night. Some of the credit should go to his mentor."

Ward grinned at Nate. "The kid's a quick study."

The detective looked toward the kitchen doorway and smiled. "That looks very inviting, Emily."

"Help yourselves, gentlemen." She set the tray down on the coffee table and settled in between Nate and Gary on the sofa.

She'd found his stash of Oreos and a proper serving plate, Nate noted. Oh, well, the Oreos were expendable. He winked at her and reached for a cookie. "Good job. Thanks."

Blakeney took a sip of coffee then a bigger one and settled back in his chair. "First off, I'm sure you all want to know about Pressey's condition. He underwent surgery at Eastern Maine Medical last night, and he's holding his own. He's not in any condition to talk yet, but when he is, we'll be there. His doctors think he'll make it." Blakeney looked around at them. "I have to say, you folks did a first-rate job, and I'm including you in that, Emily."

She smiled and looked down at her hands. "Thank you, sir."

Blakeney leaned forward. "Now, don't be modest. Both the Misses Williams have told me how you kept things calm. You talked Pressey down, it seems. You fed him, and you kept Jeanette Williams from totally losing it. And Jette . . . Well, she's a piece of work, isn't she?" He shook his head and took another sip of coffee.

"How is she doing, sir?"

"About as well as can be expected. She won't be arraigned until Monday morning."

"Can we see her?" Emily asked.

"Doubtful. Not yet."

Emily frowned. "But she doesn't have any family."

Blakeney's brow furrowed. "That's not strictly true, now, is it?"

"You mean . . ."

Nate took Emily's hand and squeezed it. "Remember how worried Mr. Williams was last night?"

Emily nodded. "I'm glad Jeanette's parents came, even though it was so late when they got here."

"Yes, and before they left to take her to the lodge, Nicholas Williams asked me if he would be allowed to visit Jette."

"That's right, Holman. Nicholas Williams is Jette's father, too. He hasn't had any contact with her for more than eighteen years, but he showed some concern for her last night, and that's encouraging. I think the authorities will let him visit Jette at the county jail. Mr. and Mrs. Williams plan to stay over at Lakeview Lodge with Jeanette until everything is cleared up."

"It's official, then?" Emily eyed him expectantly.

Blakeney nodded. "The DNA shows that both girls are his daughters. The one known now as Jeanette was the baby known as Marianne. And Jette is who you might call the 'real' Jeanette."

Nate wondered how the twins had taken that news.

"I'm glad Anton Pressey is still alive," Emily said quietly. "It would be so much more terrible for Jette if she had killed him." She turned to look at Blakeney. "Do you think they'll charge her with attempted manslaughter? I was there. He had threatened to kill both Jeanette and me several times, and he came at Jette like a grizzly bear intending to rip her apart."

"Only the prosecutor can decide that. If they find it was self-defense or justifiable homicide, she'll still have to answer for aiding and abetting him in kidnapping and terrorizing. And if we find out she knew he murdered Stella Lessard . . ."

"She didn't." Emily spoke with firm confidence. "She was just as shocked as I was when he said he'd given Stella what she had coming to her. I'm positive Jette didn't know Anton killed her until last night."

"You may have to testify to that effect," Blakeney said.

"Gladly. I'll do anything I can to help Jette. She saved my life, and Jeanette's, too, for all I know. Anton was ticked off at me, and I was afraid he'd turn around and shoot me at any second, the way he shot at Rocky through the door. If I said the wrong word . . ." Her voice caught and she looked at Nate with tears glistening in her eyes.

"That's why I didn't tell Jonathan to call the police when Jette and I went into the marina. Anton said if we didn't show up with a boat in fifteen minutes, he would shoot Jeanette, and I believe he would have."

"His own grandchild," Ward said, shaking his head.

"She meant nothing to him," Emily insisted. "I don't think he really cares about Jette, either. She was a tool for him, a way to get money. I doubt that man ever knew how to love." She sniffed and Nate slipped his arm around her.

"The D.A. is going to charge him with Mrs. Lessard's murder, right?" Gary asked.

"Absolutely." Blakeney reached for a cookie and sat back again. "We've got him cold on everything that happened yesterday, but the murder charge will be harder to prove. Emily, your testimony will be very important, and the girls' as well. I'm sure Jette Williams's lawyer is making it clear to her that testifying against Pressey will help her a great deal."

"She must be terrified." Emily shook her head. "Nate, will you see if we can get in to see her this weekend?"

"I'll do my best."

Gary set his mug on the coffee table and looked earnestly at Emily. "I rode to the county jail with her last night, and she said something kind of odd. She said, 'I guess God protected Emily after all, but what's going to happen to me now?' "

"I have to see her." Emily's blue eyes pleaded, and Nate squeezed her shoulder.

"If they'll let us, we will."

Gary smiled sheepishly. "I didn't know what to say to her, but I told her, 'Seems to me that God protected you, too, Miss Williams. He's right there all the time, waiting for you to come home.' Kind of corny, I guess."

"No, it's not," Emily said. "That's what I tried to tell her last night. God will forgive her for everything she did wrong. Pray that she'll believe that."

Blakeney cleared his throat. "Not to interrupt the prayer meeting, but there's one more thing I wanted to tell you boys. It's about the Procaine that killed Stella Lessard."

Nate's attention snapped to what the detective was saying. Ward, too, sat waiting for what Blakeney would say.

"I got word late yesterday that the state police in New Hampshire have linked Pressey to a robbery at a pharmacy in Dover a couple of months back."

"I wondered how he got it," Nate said. "It

seemed an unlikely weapon for a man like him."

Gary grimaced as he twisted open an Oreo. "Yeah, he prefers a 9 millimeter."

"It took them awhile," Blakeney told them, "but they've traced it back to him. They've been looking for him all week but couldn't find him down there. When they heard we've got him up here, they contacted us. If we ever get done with him, they'll be only too happy to prosecute him." The detective looked over at Emily and nodded. "I won't tell the other reporters that item when I do the press conference this afternoon, but you can break it in your paper on Tuesday."

Emily smiled at him. "Thank you, Detective. That's generous of you."

Blakeney shrugged. "It's not much, but you deserve some sort of break. Of course, his capture and you girls' kidnapping and safe release will be all over tonight's TV news reports and tomorrow's daily papers."

"Will you publicize Jette's arrest?" Emily asked.

"It's a matter of public record, and she was acting as an accessory."

"She did save our lives," Emily said.

Blakeney nodded thoughtfully. "You can say that in the *Journal* if you want. Make her a hero, I don't care. She came down on the right side in the end. Maybe she deserves a break, too."

As the officers left the marina house a few minutes later, Nate and Emily said goodbye on the porch, out of the rain. Emily noticed a stooped figure huddled under the eaves of the marina and poked Nate in the ribs.

He looked down at her with arched eyebrows. She pointed, and he shifted his gaze toward the store.

"Cedar. What do you suppose he's got in that sack?"

The bundle Cedar held looked more like a pillowcase than a grocery sack. Emily squinted but couldn't decide. Maybe it was a laundry bag.

"Hey, Cedar," Nate called. When the man raised his chin, Nate waved.

Blakeney and Gary were already in their cars, but Ward stopped and looked at Nate then followed his gaze. As Cedar walked slowly across the parking lot, Ward turned and ambled back to Nate's porch.

"What're you up to today, Cedar?" Ward asked.

"Come on up here out of the rain," Nate said. "What brings you to town on such a wet day?"

Cedar looked at him silently for a moment then held the sack out to him.

Nate frowned. "What's this?"

Cedar cleared his throat. "I know you're gonna say I shouldn't have done it, but I did."

The back of Emily's neck prickled.

"What did you do?" Nate asked.

Cedar nodded toward the sack. "I dug it up."

"How's that?" Nate asked.

"What are you talking about?" Ward scowled at him. "Talk sense, man."

Cedar flicked a glance at him, then looked back at Nate. "I heard them talking about digging up Stella's flower beds."

"Who?" Nate's eyebrows drew together.

Things clicked into place in Emily's mind. "Anton and Jette," she said. "When they were holding Jeanette and me at Stella's house, Cedar came around. They were talking about digging to find the cash Anton was sure Stella had hidden."

Cedar nodded, his lips pressed tightly together.

"So you went digging around afterward?" Nate asked, fixing Cedar with a glare. "You know I told you to keep away from there."

"I figured they'd find it sooner or later if I

didn't dig it up. So after you and . . . and the other officer left, well, I . . . I dug it up."

"What?" Nate demanded again.

Emily leaned closer to him and whispered, "Why don't you just look?"

Nate eyed her cautiously. "I'm not sure I want to. Could be a dead cat or anything." He turned back to Cedar. "Come on, spill it."

Cedar sighed and looked down at his soggy shoes. Clumps of wet earth clung to them. "Last year Stella wanted me to plant some hollyhocks, and I found something. She said she'd almost forgotten she hid it there. Then she kind of laughed and told me to put it back. So I did. But if that mean man was going to start digging, I didn't want him to have it. Stella said it was for somebody else."

"Who?"

"Don't know."

Slowly, Nate smoothed out the wadded neck of the sack and opened it. He stood still, staring down inside.

"What is it?" Emily asked at last.

"A soda bottle."

"What?" She made a face. "What else?"

"It's a two-liter plastic bottle."

"And something in it," Cedar said.

Nate reached into the sack and pulled the

bottle out. He held it up where everyone could see it. Mud obscured the contents, but Emily was sure it included some rolled-up papers.

"What should we do with it?" she asked.

"Probably throw it away." Nate shook his head. "I suppose we'd better take it to John Wolfe, but I can't imagine that it's anything important."

"Stella hid it a long time ago," Cedar said, nodding. "It's part of her inheritance."

"Her estate," Emily said gently. "Nate, we'd better call Mr. Wolfe."

Nate sighed. "So much for my day off."

"It's too wet to go fishing or swimming anyway," Emily said.

"I'll call him," Ward offered.

"Thanks." Nate opened the door to the house. "Come on in and get dry, Cedar. We have some cookies left, and we can make more coffee."

"Don't drink coffee," Cedar said.

"How about hot chocolate?" Emily asked.

Cedar's eyes lit. "Sometimes."

She grasped his sleeve. "Come on. I'll make you some."

John Wolfe and his wife arrived forty minutes later. "I hope you don't mind that I brought Brenda," he told Nate.

"No problem." Nate introduced Emily,

Ward, and Cedar.

"It was too wet to work in the garden," Mrs. Wolfe said.

Emily chuckled.

Nate said under his breath, "Tell that to Cedar."

She elbowed him. "Won't you sit down, Mr. and Mrs. Wolfe? I've made fresh coffee."

"Oh, no thanks," Wolfe said. "But if you want to bring out the item Mr. Sproul found, I'll take a look."

Nate brought the sack and handed it to Wolfe. "I spread out some newspapers on the coffee table so you can put it there. There seems to be a piece of paper rolled up inside. Thought you might want to cut the bottle open." He eyed Wolfe's immaculate clothing and added, "Or I could do it for you if you want."

"Thank you. I may take you up on that." Wolfe held the bottle up by its lid, using only his fingertips. "Hard to tell what it is, with the label and all the dirt." He tipped the bottle upside down, and something slid down near the cap. "Looks like something metallic. Here, Nate, why don't you go ahead and cut it open, if you've got the tools."

Nate braced the bottle on the coffee table

and sliced into it with his pocketknife. He cut completely around the middle of the bottle and pulled the two halves apart, spilling the contents on the newspapers. A small photograph lay face up, and Wolfe reached for it, momentarily ignoring the rolled-up paper and other items.

"A cute baby." He turned the photo over. "Lois, age one." He passed the photo to his wife and reached for the paper. "And this appears to be Lois Pressey's birth certificate. This sheet of paper says, 'for Lois.' " He poked at the small items that lay on the newspaper. "A necklace and earrings."

"Could that be the jewelry she mentioned in her will?" Emily asked.

"Anything's possible. She specified diamond jewelry. I wonder if they're genuine." Wolfe picked up one of the earrings. "Could be diamonds. We'll have these appraised and entered into the list of contents in the estate."

"She obviously wanted Lois to have them," Emily said.

"Who's Lois?" Cedar asked. "Is that the one you were looking for?"

"Yes," Wolfe told him. "Lois was Stella Lessard's daughter. Remember, we talked about that? How she would be about forty years old now? But Lois died two years ago."

Emily reached to touch the sleeve of Cedar's plaid flannel shirt. "The man you saw at Stella's last night was her first husband, and the two girls who were there with him and me are Lois's children. They're Stella's granddaughters."

"Even that one with all the metal in her face?"

Emily smiled. "Yes, she's the one who calls herself Jette."

"Maybe she'll get these." Cedar poked one of the earrings with his finger.

"She may indeed," Wolfe said.

"Why do you suppose she buried them in a bottle?" Brenda Wolfe asked.

Emily stirred and glanced at Nate. He nodded, as though telling her to go ahead. "I think she wanted to be sure her second husband never saw them," she said. "From all indications, Edgar Lessard never knew about Stella's daughter or her former life. She didn't want to destroy these things. The birth certificate and picture were proof that Lois was her daughter. And perhaps she hoped that Lois would get the necklace and earrings one day. I suspect those are things Stella saved from her former life, with Anton Pressey."

"In which case, they may have been stolen," Nate added.

"True."

"Probably impossible to find out after all these years," Wolfe said. He stood and gathered the items. "I'll take these to the office and lock them up. Thank you for bringing them in, Mr. Sproul. I'm sure Mrs. Lessard's granddaughters will be grateful."

Nate clapped Cedar on the shoulder. "It was good of you to do that."

The old man shrugged. "She said it was for someone else. I didn't know who."

Wolfe nodded gravely. "I'll tell the Williams girls what you did."

"So . . . they're gonna get the house?" Cedar asked.

"It looks that way. Of course, one of the young women is in jail at the moment." Wolfe gritted his teeth. "She can't inherit if she's found to be guilty in her grandmother's murder."

Emily's heart sped up and she stepped toward the attorney. "Is she even being charged in Stella's death? I'm sure she didn't know it was a homicide."

"The district attorney will decide what the charges are. We'll know after the arraignment on Monday."

"Are you representing her?" Nate asked.

Wolfe shook his head. "I don't generally represent criminal defendants. And anyway,

I'm the official representative of the estate, which could be a conflict. The court will appoint an attorney, I imagine."

Tears pricked Emily's eyes. "I hope she gets a good one."

22

Emily shivered as they passed through the metal detector at the Penobscot County Jail. *It's no worse than the one at the airport,* she told herself.

Right. Who am I kidding?

She'd visited Rocky Vigue here when he was arrested the summer before and found the place depressing. Thinking of Jette caged up here — a nineteen-year-old girl whose family had been ripped away from her — sent shudders down Emily's spine.

"You okay?" Nate reached for her hand.

She nodded and squeezed his warm fingers. She was glad he'd worn his uniform. The guards were all smiles and friendly greetings today.

Jette was already in the small interview room when they entered. She sat alone at a table, and a female guard stood near the door. Emily was glad they could meet here in relative privacy, not in the larger facility where prisoners met their families during visiting hours.

Jette's dark hair lay limp and lifeless. Her face seemed pinker than usual, and her brown eyes had shrunk to normal size without her customary heavy makeup. Her earrings, lip, and brow rings were missing. The snake tattoo circling her wrist and the flowers tattooed on her neck seemed the only remaining expressions of her individuality.

"Jette, how are you?" Emily moved across the room and embraced the girl. The guard shifted her position and watched them carefully but did not interfere.

"I'm okay." Her voice cracked, and her eyes swam with sudden tears.

"Oh, honey, I'm sorry." Emily drew her close again.

Jette sobbed. "How long will I be here? No one tells me anything."

"I don't know."

Nate cleared his throat. "You're going down the street for your arraignment this morning. Did they tell you that?"

She nodded. "I don't know what that means, though."

Emily patted her shoulder. "You'll go into the courtroom, and someone will read the charges against you. If you can't afford a lawyer, the judge will appoint one."

"Several lawyers have volunteered to represent you," Nate added. "Your case has caught the public eye, so to speak. You may get to take your pick."

Jette gulped. "I don't guess I can afford anything right now. I spent all my savings on this trip. I was hoping Grandma had left me something, but now I don't guess I'll get it if she did."

"Your attorney can advise you on that," Nate said, "but I think you can still inherit, even if you're indicted for a crime. It . . . all depends on what the charges are."

As long as you didn't murder the person leaving you an inheritance, Emily thought, but she didn't put it in words. "Just tell the truth, no matter what they ask you," she said.

"I didn't do anything." Jette's voice squeaked as she gazed pleadingly at Emily. Tears bathed her cheeks. "I never meant for anyone to get hurt, especially not Grandpa."

"I know." Emily smoothed her hair back. Nate surprised her by producing a folded cotton handkerchief and handing it to Jette.

"How's he doing?" Jette sniffed and dabbed at her eyes. "No one will tell me."

"He had surgery Friday," Nate said. "They said yesterday he was conscious. I called the hospital this morning, and he's stable now."

Jette let out a pent-up breath. "That's good, I guess."

"Yes." Nate pulled out a chair for Emily next to Jette. She sat down, and he went around the table.

"So . . . the police will be questioning him now, I suppose."

Nate nodded. "Detective Blakeney visited him yesterday, and he intends to see him again today."

"Will they keep me in jail because I sh– shot him?"

"You saved my life, Jette." Emily stroked her hand, trying not to look at the snake on her wrist, with its fangs bared, ready to strike. "I believe Anton would have killed me, and maybe Jeanette, too. He would have been furious when he realized the police weren't going to let him escape. I can't thank you enough for what you did. And I'll make sure the district attorney knows that."

Jette hauled in a shuddering breath. "It's so scary. The people here aren't very nice."

Tears gushed into Emily's eyes. "Are you sure you're all right?"

Jette ducked her head. "The woman they put me with — Sheila — she's not bad. She stole some money from the office where she worked. But some of them —" She looked up into Emily's face with bloodshot eyes. "Did you know there's a woman here who killed her own baby? And one who killed her boyfriend's new girlfriend."

Emily pulled her into a brief hug. "I'm so sorry you have to be here. We'll pray that it will be over soon."

"Do you really pray for me, or are you just saying that?"

"We pray for you every day. Lots of times every day." Emily looked to Nate for confirmation.

"Em and I prayed for you together right before we came in here," he said. "We hope you'll understand how much God cares about you. Even though you're in an awful place right now, He's here to take care of you."

"I did get a cellmate who's not mean," Jette admitted. "She cries a lot. It's hard to sleep at night because she's always bawling."

"But you're safe?" Emily asked.

Jette gave a tentative nod. "When you go to eat or take a shower, it's kind of scary with all these women around."

"They don't bring your meals to you?"

"No. Those are the worst times — when we're in a group and I don't know when someone's going to push me or something. I asked the guard to stay close while I took my shower this morning. She was kind of crabby, and she kept saying, 'Hurry up,' but she stayed."

"That's good," Emily said.

"There's one more thing." Nate leaned toward her across the table. "The results of the DNA tests are in, and they prove that you and Jeanette are Stella Lessard's granddaughters. It's official. John Wolfe is going to announce it today. You and Jeanette will inherit equally if your court case goes well."

Jette puffed out a breath and stared at the opposite wall. "Twins?"

"Yes," Nate said.

She shook her head. "Jeanette hates me."

Emily shot a glance at Nate, and he grimaced. "You know, in time you might discover that you have a lot in common," she said. "If not, then it's all right not to force a relationship. But you are sisters. There's no doubt."

"Jette, your father asked if he could see you, and they've told him to come this afternoon, after you've had your arraignment."

She jerked upright in her chair and stared at him. "Are you sure?"

Emily smiled at her. "We saw him yesterday. He'd tried to see you twice already. He told us he would come this afternoon, no matter what happens in court. And if they'll let him, he'll be in the courtroom this morning."

"Really?"

"Really. He wants to get to know you."

Nate leaned his elbows on the table. "Would you mind if we prayed now, Jette?"

She hesitated, then nodded. "Okay. Can't hurt."

Emily bowed her head as Nate said quietly, "Lord, we thank You for preserving Jette and Emily and Jeanette. We thank You for Jette's family, and we ask that if it's in Your plan, she can form a good relationship with the Williamses. We pray for Your will to be done in Jette's life. Give her courage as she goes to court today and the faith to believe in You. And we ask, too, that You will heal Anton and let him stand trial. Let justice be done for his crimes."

Emily added her amen to Nate's.

Jette smiled through her tears. "Thanks. I can't believe my father really wants to see me. He's not going to yell at me, is he?"

"No, honey." Emily squeezed her hand.

A man opened the door and looked in.

"Time's up. Williams, we'll be transporting you to the courthouse now."

Emily and Nate stood.

The guard came forward and took Jette's arm. "Come with me. I'll process you out. A state trooper will go with you in the van."

"Thank you," Jette called to Nate and Emily as they headed for the door.

When they reached the street, Emily looked toward where they'd parked Nate's SUV.

"Look." She tugged Nate's sleeve. "It's Jeanette."

They hurried toward the young woman, and she advanced to meet them on the sidewalk.

"Hi. They wouldn't let me in."

"I'm sorry." Emily gave her a quick hug. "They're taking Jette to the courthouse now. Maybe you'll get to see her after."

"My dad's over there." Jeanette blinked and choked back a sob. "Seems like he and Mom and I talked all weekend. Mom left this morning to pick up my brothers and my little sister from Grandma Smith's. But we've all agreed, if Jette will let us, we want to be her family."

Nate's eyes lit up. "That's great."

"It sure is," Emily said. "She's a little nervous about how you and your family will think about her and act toward her. When we told her your father was planning to go to the arraignment and visit her afterward, she was touched."

Jeanette swallowed hard. "I'm not sure if we'll ever be close like sisters should . . ."

Emily smiled. "I'm told sisters argue now and then."

"Oh, yeah." Jeanette chuckled. "That's true. Anyway, I'm going to try."

"I'm glad."

"I'm going to start reading the Bible, too. The pastor was really nice yesterday. He spent quite a while with us at the lodge." Jeanette looked up at Nate, flushing slightly. "I like your mom, too."

"Isn't she great?" Nate asked. "I'm glad you and your parents came to church."

"We're going to start going every week," Jeanette said. "Your pastor told us a good one to go to near where we live. And he said we can hold a memorial service for Grandma Stella at your church after we know what's going to happen with Jette."

"That sounds like a good idea." Emily looked at her watch. "Say, Nate, we'd better get over to the courthouse."

"You're going to the arraignment, too?" Jeanette looked at Emily in surprise.

"We want to support Jette." Emily smiled at her. "She can use all the friends she can get today. Nate has to work at three o'clock, so we have to head home by noon, but if her case comes up before then, we'll be there. Would you like to walk over with us?"

"Sure. Thanks."

Jeanette and Emily fell into step with Nate close behind them.

"This has been a rough time for your family," Emily said, "but you'll get through it and be stronger because of it."

Jeanette smiled. "Dad's been great this weekend. He's going to Mr. Wolfe's office with me this afternoon, after he goes to see Jette. We'll drive home in my car. Mom took his." She looked over at Emily. "I don't know why I thought he didn't love me."

"You don't have to worry about that. It's obvious he and your mom both care very much about you."

Jeanette nodded. "We all agreed we'll try to share that love with Jette." She bobbed her head to one side and winced. "I guess I have to get used to a new name. Do I look like a Marianne to you?"

Emily smiled and squeezed her shoulders. "You've lived as Jeanette so long, you may want to keep using that as a nickname."

"Maybe I'll ask Jette if she minds. At least she got a nickname that goes with her personality."

Epilogue

The morning of Emily and Nate's wedding, the sky was gray and a mist hovered over Blue Heron Lake.

"Don't worry about the weather," said Carol Gillespie as she pinned her daughter's veil in place. "The weatherman said it will clear up. I'm sure the sun will be shining by the time the ceremony's over."

"I hope so. Otherwise we'll have to take pictures inside."

There was a tap on the door of the small Sunday school room that served as a dressing room for Emily and her attendants.

"Come in," Carol called.

Gary poked his head through the doorway. "We're ready to seat the mothers."

Emily smiled. "Go on, Mom. Everyone's waiting." She gave her mother a quick hug. "See you in a minute!"

A few moments later Emily met her uncle Waldo in the vestry. She blinked back tears at the sight of him in his tuxedo. *If only Dad could be here, too.*

"You look fabulous, Emmy." He smiled and stooped to kiss her cheek.

"Thanks. Are you ready?" she whispered.

"Am *I* ready?" Uncle Waldo chuckled softly. "Ready whenever you are."

"I've been ready for a long time!" She beamed up at him. "Thanks for walking me down the aisle. I know Dad would be happy having you stand in for him."

"My pleasure." He offered her his arm.

A second later, the pianist began playing Pachelbel's Canon and the congregation rose as they started down the aisle. Emily could see Nate standing at the front of the church with Pastor Phillips, Gary, and Jeff Lewis. Her own attendants, Felicia and Raven, also stood at the front. Raven could have been a model in her chic sapphire gown. Though Felicia didn't have the same ease and natural beauty, the style also suited her, and she'd opted for a sleek new haircut and contact lenses to replace her glasses. Emily's friends looked their best today.

The church was full. Their smiling faces filled Emily's mind with memories as she and her uncle walked with measured steps to the front. Besides church members and regular summer island residents including the Vigues and the Kimmels, many Baxter residents had accepted the invitation to celebrate with Nate and Emily. Cedar Sproul slouched in the back pew, and Charlie Benton, Bridget Kaplin, and Rita Eliot sat together just behind Jon and Allison Woods, who had closed the marina for the afternoon. A handful of Emily's old school friends and a dozen family members — cousins, aunts, and uncles — filled the two pews behind Carol. The church members and staff of Lakeview Lodge spilled over the back half of both the "bride's" and the "groom's" sides. The sprinkling of law enforcement uniforms told Emily that Ward Delaney, Orson Blakeney, and several other officers had come to support Nate.

Jeanette and Jette sat together just behind Nate's family, at his request. Emily was glad the sisters had decided to come. And were those Stella's diamond earrings Jette was wearing, and her necklace around Jeanette's neck?

Emily's mother was already crying, and as they reached the altar, Emily caught Connie Phillips's eye and saw that she was near tears as well.

I was fine until they started crying, Emily thought. She laughed to herself as she felt the tears coming on. Everyone was so happy for them. And then her eyes met Nate's again. She didn't think he'd ever looked happier.

As Pastor Phillips opened in prayer and welcomed the guests to the ceremony, Emily offered up a quick prayer of thanksgiving of her own. "God, thank You so much for bringing Nate and me together again, and for giving us to each other. Help us to love each other and to love You more."

After taking their vows, Emily and Nate mingled with their guests at the reception, held outside at the public boat landing and picnic area. The sun had indeed come out, shimmering on the lake. The time spent with friends and family they didn't often get to see was all too short. Nate lifted Emily to stand on one of the picnic tables and throw her bouquet. She tossed it to the cluster of women and watched with delight as Raven surfaced from the melee holding the pink roses.

"We need to leave soon," Nate whispered as he lifted her back to earth. "My mom says we'd better cut the cake and then go over to the house to change."

Before they left the boat landing, Emily took a moment to single out the twins.

"Thanks for coming." She smiled and gave them each a hug.

"Thanks for inviting us," said Jette. Emily thought she looked cute, though a little mismatched in the diamond drop earrings, a pair of black satin pants, and a glittery purple and silver tank top. Jeanette's sweeter look, a pink-and-yellow-flowered sundress, tallied with her more traditional taste, and Emily wondered how much their differences were due to their upbringing.

"You've been really kind to both of us through everything," said Jeanette. "I'm glad we could be friends."

Emily looked from one sister to the other. They didn't seem so annoyed at being in the same place at the same time anymore, and she hoped that perhaps the two of them might get to be friends after all.

"Did you decide what to do with your grandmother's house?" she asked.

The twins looked at each other and smiled.

Jeanette said, "Since Jette is on probation, our dad is responsible for her now. She's staying with us, and we've talked about the house a lot."

Jette nodded. "We're going to sell it. We both like Baxter, but we decided the money will be more useful to us. We can both go to the state university if we want and get some education."

"That sounds great," Emily said.

Jeanette shrugged with a sheepish smile. "We think so. I'm going to take some classes in early childhood education."

"And I'm thinking about studying art."

"Sounds like a good plan."

Nate came and took her by the hand. "Sorry, Em, but we really do have to leave."

"Where are you going?" Jette asked.

Nate grinned. "It's a big secret. But the first stop is the Bangor airport."

They hurried to the marina house to change. Nate had their luggage already packed in his SUV. When they came out, the guests had gathered in the marina parking lot. Mr. and Mrs. Nathan Pierce Holman drove out in a cascade of birdseed and good wishes. Emily sat back and sighed with contentment as she watched her husband drive toward the airport. She thought to herself, *This is for the rest of our lives.*

ABOUT THE AUTHORS

Susan Page Davis is the author of more than twenty novels. She and her husband, Jim, live in beautiful Maine. Both are active in a small, independent Baptist church. Their six children range in age from fifteen to thirty-two. When possible, they enjoy spending time with their six far-flung grandchildren. Susan has homeschooled all of her children. She enjoys reading, genealogy, needlework, and meeting her readers. Visit her Web site at: www.susanpagedavis.com.

Megan Elaine Davis grew up in rural Maine, where she was homeschooled with her five siblings. She holds a bachelor's degree in creative writing from Bob Jones University and has published poetry, articles, and humorous anecdotes in various publications. Besides writing, she enjoys reading, traveling, theater, cooking, and chatting with friends. Her favorite authors are Agatha Christie, Jane Austen, and C. S. Lewis. *Impostors at Blue Heron Lake* is her third novel. She recently became Mrs. John-Mark Cullen and now resides in England.

You may correspond with these authors by writing:
Susan Page Davis and/or
Megan Elaine Davis
Author Relations
PO Box 721
Uhrichsville, OH 44683

The employees of Thorndike Press hope you have enjoyed this Large Print book. All our Thorndike, Wheeler, and Kennebec Large Print titles are designed for easy reading, and all our books are made to last. Other Thorndike Press Large Print books are available at your library, through selected bookstores, or directly from us.

For information about titles, please call:
(800) 223-1244

or visit our Web site at:
http://gale.cengage.com/thorndike

To share your comments, please write:
Publisher
Thorndike Press
295 Kennedy Memorial Drive
Waterville, ME 04901